CURSE RAIDER

IRISH MYSTIC LEGENDS BOOK TWO

JENNIFER ROSE MCMAHON

Cover design by Rebecca Frank

Edited by Naomi Hughes

Dubhdara Publishing

To Maggie
For your friendship and fierce loyalty

BOOK TWO

CURSE RAIDER

by Jennifer Rose McMahon

CHAPTER 1

And now, I was a million miles away.

Swiping at the thick fog that blurred my vision, I stared into the perfect clarity of the bright blue sky. The smoke-like curtain parted for a brief moment, allowing me to see across the choppy Irish sea to far-off, rolling green hills but then the shroud closed again. It wasn't the weather causing the impenetrable haze though. It was my clouded, drugged mind.

Startled by my own self-awareness, I sucked in my breath as if waking from a shocking dream. I turned around to take in my surroundings and in an instant it came crashing down on me.

Lucidity.

And the haunting reality of my situation.

A glorious Irish landscape sprawled across the horizon beyond the vast stretch of sea, but looming behind me were the stark gray exterior walls of my prison. Memory of who I was flooded me while vile sickness rose in my throat. I'd been imprisoned against my will for rehabilitation—or cleansing, as some called it. I'd started to lose track of time as each day bled into the next in a morphed time warp.

I wouldn't let them drug me again. I couldn't. It was my only chance at holding on to myself and getting off this island prison.

I didn't belong here.

None of us did.

But there was no hope of changing the minds of my captors. The witch hunt led by God-fearing believers had convinced everyone I danced with the devil. Only my closest circle, the other gifted ones, knew the truth. They called it second sight.

I was a seer.

Closing my eyes, I focused on my visions—the wind, the weightlessness, and the things I saw during my episodes. But no matter how hard I concentrated, I couldn't conjure a new event—one that would transport me away from this captivity. And of all times, now was when I needed one the most.

I kicked at the sand beneath my feet, frustrated from not being able to use my gift. Looking back over my shoulder, I glanced around, fighting the feeling of being watched. My captors rarely let me out of their sight, and now they were likely searching for me.

Had I sent a note for help? Maybe more than once. Or had that been a dream? I vaguely remembered sneaking a note onto the ferry that visited the island each week, but the details floated through my head, lost in the haze.

It was the haze of my drug induced stupor. It had shut down all vision and I remained lost in the confines of this horrid, abusive corrections facility. Locked away from society for quiet reflection and prayer, it was enough to make me truly insane. Or in their minds, more insane.

It certainly wasn't difficult to see why the local superstitious folk, led by Sister Margaret and Mrs. Flannery, were intimidated by me—always staring into oblivion in random trances, rambling of time travel, and embarking on a never-ending search through castle ruins for a friend lost in the abyss. They were the ones responsible for having me sanctioned here.

But there was a lot more to their aggressive actions than concern over my mental wellbeing. They intended to stop not only me, but all of the gifted ones. And somehow, they knew I was the key to the success of their extermination crusade. I just didn't know how, or why, but I was determined to find the answers.

I stared at the solemn gray building, once a retreat for monks long ago, and a shiver ran through me. Inside it held a variety of broken teenage girls, some truly unwell and others becoming unwell from the cold-hearted treatment of the uncaring, stoic nurses within. Tired nuns ran the place, biding their time as part of their duty to 'helping others', but most seemed to have lost their souls while waiting for their transfer to the next, more glamorous, mission.

My eyes widened as the fresh air entering my lungs purged whatever haze was left in my brain and I stood taller.

Now was my chance.

This brief moment of clarity gave me the chance to escape and there was no time to second guess the unexpected gift. Scanning the edge of the lapping water and then focusing out to sea, I considered the limitations of the small island with only one building, no boat, and a single purpose.

Captivity.

Too far to swim, it would be certain death to even try. I grabbed my hair in clenched panic. Think, Izzy, think.

I scoured the beach. Driftwood. Broken crab trap. Rope.

I shook my head in doubt at the usefulness of my random scavenged bits. But there had to be something better, like a hidden boat somewhere, for emergencies. I tore around the bend of the coast for a better view in search of a secret dock or maybe a shed.

"Stop right there. Not another step!" A wicked voice shot me point-blank in my back. "Sanctions. More demerits for wanderin' beyond the approved borders of the home." Then a sickening laugh. "Keep it up, girleen, and you'll have no privileges left whatsoever."

I spun around in terror and locked eyes with Sister Francis.

She approached with a sinister smirk that sent a clear flight message through my shaking bones.

I was in real danger, and it stood right in front of me.

~

Her eyes narrowed with each step closer, calculating what she would do with the opportunity I'd presented to her—how she might torture me this time. My death gaze made no attempt at hiding my contempt for her arrogant control over me, and likely fueled her evil planning.

"You'll have yer meals alone now. Can't be trusted. Ya shan't be given any freedoms here forward. Sure, look at ya, gazing out across the sea. Thinkin' of a swim perhaps?"

My spine straightened. "No, I, I just needed some fresh air. I didn't mean to wander so far."

The clarity in my mind forced me to remain compliant and apologetic, even though my civility caused me to grind on my molars in frustration. If I was careful enough, I'd be able to appear overmedicated, so not to raise any alarm that I might actually be thinking for myself. Drooped eyes and slow speech might help make my escape possible.

I scratched my head and looked around like I was lost. "I'm not really sure how I got out here. I think I might need a rest."

"Ya don't fool me, child." She stepped closer, peering into my eyes. "Ya look rather bright eyed ta me, like a sly fox."

Her cold words sent panic through my heart. She held no care or affection for me, or for any of us, refusing to ever call us by name and then referring to me only as 'child' or 'girleen'. It was her attempt at making me feel unimportant and needy. It was even more frustrating for me because at eighteen, I was light years ahead of most my age with what felt like lifetimes of formidable experience.

I had to get off the island before it was too late. Before I lost touch with who I was—before I got transformed into a lobotomized zombie. Or worse, had my spirit broken and became a conforming simpleton.

I also had to keep faith that Ryan would still be trying to get me out of here as well. I just had to believe that.

"Really, I think I just need a rest," I said again.

"And a rest is what you'll get. We won't be allowin' any of yer carry-on here, in a house of worship. Ya won't be conjuring the beast or speakin' with anyone in the beyond. Not while yer here under my watch."

Oh my god. She was drinking the Kool-Aid too. She believed every word of the angry mob who wanted to cleanse their town of its magic-wielding misfits. I pictured the torches and pitchforks that danced in her mind and I was shaken by her simplicity.

My visions made me misunderstood, that was for sure. They made me look like a freak to those who feared the unknown. Ryan and his grandmother, Maureen, were the same. But we meant no harm, keeping to ourselves.

Our kind once held honorable labels, like mystic and wise-ones, but that had all changed somehow. Now we were targeted for being different, like we were a threat to their rigid social order.

"Let's go!" She yanked at my arm. "Time fer yer medicine."

I stumbled along the path with her roughly tugging at my wrist. Every fiber of my being begged to pull away and run, but there was nowhere to go. And I knew my best chance was to play along and fly under the radar as just another compliant patient. The thought of being medicated again made me panic though.

"I'm sure I'll be fine once I have a nap. I really don't think I need any medicine, thank you." My voice caught in my constricting throat.

"Mmhm. Ya really think we'd have any control at all 'round here without the help of yer meds? Come on, now, girl. Ya must be smarter than that." She pushed me through the rusted metal door at the front entrance. "To the infirmary."

My mind raced, planning how I would avoid swallowing any pills she gave to me. I was certain the first check would be under my tongue, so up at my gums inside my cheek would be better. I just couldn't remember how they actually checked to be sure the meds were taken and prayed this plan would work.

We pushed through the white door into the infirmary and I caught a glimpse of Jayne—my one friend here. Well, sort of. We were both out of it most of the time but every once in a while we'd have eye contact at just the right moment and laugh our asses off at the absurdity of our situations. Kindred spirits in hell.

But at the moment, Jayne was not well. She slumped in her chair with her head propped against the wall. Drool trickled down her chin and her eyes stared off at nothing. My heart rate accelerated ten-fold.

Please God. Don't let that happen to me.

Begging for God's help was always an indicator of true fear for me. And that idea alone sent my alarm to a higher point.

"Take this." Sister Francis handed me a cup of orange juice then turned back to the nurse behind the counter. Whatever meds the nurse was collecting, I was sure they would be my doom.

My mind shot into overdrive. If I drank the juice before I got the pills, then I could put the pills in my mouth and pretend to drink them down. Fake swallows would allow me time to press the pills up between my cheek and gums. In an instant of quick thinking, I gulped down the juice.

Holding the cup with my fingers wrapped around it, I hid the fact that it was now empty and waited for the pills.

Sister Francis turned to me with her eyebrows lifted and just stared. She watched me like she was waiting for me to say something or do something.

So I asked, "Are you going to give me the medicine now?"

She chuckled and looked at the nurse with an arrogant grin. As she turned back to me, her smirk pulled up higher on her cheeks. It stretched up beyond her eyes as her face trailed into a blur of colors. Her voice morphed into a slow, sickening sound as she spoke to me.

"Sure, ya just drank it."

CHAPTER 2

The echoing blast of a fog horn jolted me straight up in my bed. Blinking away the sleepy haze in my eyes, I wondered if the fog horn was a dream or if it was my own subconscious attempt at tearing me from my juice-induced stupor.

I glanced across the uniform rows of metal beds—girls still sleeping, unaffected by the reverberating sound of the sunrise horn that filled every space.

All the girls were sleeping, except one. Jayne.

She remained lying down, but her eyes locked onto mine, calculating our next moves through the space between us. The wheels of her mind displayed their complex turning through her piercing eyes and she latched onto me like we were the only two scheming people on the island. And she was probably right.

Her eyes moved to the window above my head and then back to me. I scrambled to my knees and looked out. With a quick nod, I confirmed her suspicion—the arrival of the Sunday morning ferry, the one that carried the priest to the island for distribution of holy communion.

My stomach turned at the thought of taking communion. Not because I had given up on the church long ago, but more so because of the arrogant stares and pompous chagrin that laced the gazes of the staff. They believed we were sinners whose penance was measured and cleansed each Sunday by this visit. My head shook in frustrated annoyance and Jayne grinned.

Her half-smile lit up her face and her natural beauty was impossible to miss—large blue eyes, jet black shining hair and full lips. And her striking beauty was the cause of her untimely downfall.

The attention Jayne received from the boys in her village was enough to raise suspicion among the locals that they may have a harlot in their midst. Ridiculous. But, more unfortunate, Jayne attracted the attention of grown men as well, some married, and the women of her town banded together. They forced her family to send her away for rehabilitation from being a whore...or becoming one, just to be safe.

At seventeen, Jayne had never even had her first kiss and now here she was, rotting away her youth for the sins of others. My fists clenched at the absurdity and I vowed to get her out of this prison and back into the real world where she belonged. A world where she could live free again.

I pulled my covers off and dropped my bare feet on the cold tile floor. Jayne's eyebrows lifted as she watched me. We weren't supposed to rise until given permission but any time my brain was thinking for itself, I took advantage of the opportunity.

I waved my hand for Jayne to follow me.

We tiptoed across the room, careful to not disturb the other girls. Some of them had been brainwashed far enough that they actually complied with the rules and ratted out any offenders. It was like they thought they belonged here and it was good for them. Like they believed Jayne and I were the trouble-makers because we thought for ourselves, when we could. And we got punished for it on a regular basis. It wasn't much different from school as I thought about the social order more—they were teacher's pets and we were their targets, the non-conforming rebels.

"What are we doing, Izzy? You're insane," Jayne whispered.

"It's a boat. We need to see if there's any way to sneak on and hide.

They'll take us back to the mainland and we can run," I whispered back, reaching for her to come closer.

I turned the knob of our dormitory door and it clunked in its housing, causing us both to freeze. Scanning the sleeping girls for any alarm blowers—one shifted but then fell silent again—we turned back to the door. Jayne chewed on her lower lip as I turned the knob again and it popped open.

Standing motionless for a moment, we stared into each other's eyes in panic of rousing any of the girls, but then, certain they remained unaffected, we snuck out into the cold corridor. Creeping along the dim, antiseptic hallway, we moved toward the door that led out to the back of the institution.

"We're dead if they catch us." Jayne jabbed at my ribs. "I swear to God, I can't spend another day in solitary, praying for forgiveness. That huge crucifix creeps me the hell out."

"It's better than having to wash miles of sheets by hand. That's exquisite torture at its finest," I blasted back at her, as quietly as I could. "I never want to see another sheet as long as I live."

She chuckled. "No shit. I swear they make us do that just to drive us crazy. I mean, who washes their sheets everyday? When I get out of here, I vow to wash my sheets like once a year!"

A laugh threatened to burst out of my mouth and I caught it in my nose, making it sound like a stifled sneeze. Both of us turned red with silent laughter that we struggled to suppress. Hands on knees, we gasped for air through our quaking shudders.

"Come on, harlot." I pulled on her. "Follow me." I pushed open the heavy door and fresh early morning air circulated around us.

She shoved me out the opening. "Who you callin' harlot, devil's bitch!"

I punched at her arm. "Someone forgot to say her rosary this morning," I murmured with a silent chuckle.

After propping the door open an inch with an oblong rock, I pointed in the direction of the boat, which was hidden from view just around the side of the home. Jayne hooked her arm around mine and we moved along the side of the building, hugging close to the wall for cover.

As we reached the front corner, we peered around it and caught a glimpse of a small group disembarking from the ferry. Three nuns in traditional dresses and full-coverage habits walked alongside the priest who stepped forward to greet the head of the facility, Sister Mary Carmel. Her pinched face and permanent scowl turned my blood cold and my flight response trembled, at the ready.

I turned back to Jayne. "Once they're inside, we can move closer for a better look. The ferryman will need to be distracted when..."

Jayne's sudden silence perplexed me and I followed her frozen line of vision in the direction we came from.

"Shit," we hissed in unison.

Meek Theresa-the-Snitch peered out from behind the propped door and in our distraction, we'd lost sight of Sister Francis, who'd been standing by Sister Mary Carmel. But not for long. Within seconds, Her Evilness barreled toward us, habit flapping behind her from the wind off the sea, vengeance hanging heavy on her brow. My stomach flipped over and I grabbed onto Jayne with all my strength.

The heavy door of purgatory slammed shut, leaving me in haunting silence. The familiar room sent chills up my spine. Its nickname described its lost limbo perfectly—it had a single chair, metal school desk with paper for journaling, or more like writing repentance of my sins for their sick amusement, and a small locked second-story window just above the stiff, musty cot. Madness threatened me from every blank wall, allowing focus only on the life-like crucifix, blood and all, and my molars ground together at the heartless abuse from the staff here.

Staring at a white wall, I waited for further sentencing. I pictured Jayne trapped in a similar hell and guilt poisoned my insides for bringing her into this.

But I'd never stop trying. And I knew she wouldn't either. We had to get out of this place.

Time stretched into immeasurable length as I stood in the center of the room. Waiting.

Then my ears shifted to the sound of several hard-heeled footsteps plodding down the hall. My heart rate quickened at the hope of the salvation of human contact in any form, even if it was only Sister Francis.

All fell silent for a moment and panic rose in me as fear of being left alone any longer quaked my starved soul. But then the sound of a key in the lock sent my mind soaring.

As the door pushed open, I stood taller. Sister Francis entered first, followed by one of the visiting nuns and the priest.

"Yer ta take yer communion, missy," Sister Francis stated without any emotion or eye contact.

My worried eyes darted to the priest's, begging silently for his help. But he avoided me as well, almost like he refused to acknowledge an actual person stood before him. My heart plummeted to my feet in despair at my lonely isolation.

As he lifted the host, stating, "Body of Christ," I pressed my lips together in defiance and turned my head away.

Unexpectedly, my eyes met a compassionate gaze from the visiting nun. She held me in her steady watch and as her head lifted, light shone into the shadow of her habit, illuminating her face fully. A gasp threatened to launch from my throat as shock overwhelmed me.

Mother Maureen!

Oh my god. It was Mother Maureen.

Her lips pushed out in a shushing motion and she looked down again.

How did she get in here? My heart burst with excitement at seeing her and the hope of seeing Ryan again.

She must have received the note. I must have actually sent it. Thank god!

I looked back at the priest and this time responded, "Amen," and lifted my hands for the host. Placing it in my mouth and motioning the sign of the cross, I lowered my eyes in feigned prayer.

Barely able to contain myself, I avoided eye contact with Sister Francis. She huffed and turned to the door to leave. The priest followed her and Mother Maureen positioned herself last.

In a moment that passed within two seconds, we connected in communication that spanned an eternity.

"Time to go, Isobel. Take this." She reached into her pocket and pulled a long chain out of it. Holding my eyes as the necklace twirled from her fingers, she communicated every sorrow of not getting to me sooner, every ache her grandson endured in my absence, and the despair of my aging grandmother who cried for me every day.

Then her eyes turned to strength and vigor, passing on to me the urgency of my escape. She pressed the necklace into my hand and I squeezed the heavy object that dangled from it. She turned and left the room without another word and the door slammed behind her.

As the lock clicked back into place, I remained standing in the middle of the room and my eyes grew wide with the wonder of what lay hidden in my palm. My heart rate accelerated to near lift-off as my mind flew into overdrive.

The shape and weight of the object in my hand left no doubt of Maureen's gift.

The key to reawakening my visions.

The one opportunity to generate my ability to travel through my gift of second sight—to transport me out of here.

The mystical ring of the ancient pirate queen.

The best part of being trapped in purgatory was the neglect. The isolation of the prayer room gave me a chance to think and plan my escape, and even better, my head was clear. I was free from the sedating meds they used when I wasn't quarantined.

My hand squeezed tight around the ring of the pirate queen as I considered its mystical energy. It was a connection to the past, dating back to Grace O'Malley, clan chieftain of the 1500's and Maeve's ancestor.

The last time I held the ring, it had transported me to the time of the Great Famine, and into the dungeons of Westport House where I'd seen an apparition of Maeve. Her existence had shifted to the time of Grace O'Malley's reign and she lived on in the past, in that realm.

The power of the ring combined with the force of my visions created vast uncertainty. There was no way for me to understand the full possibilities of unleashing its complex witchery, but it was my only chance at escaping from the island.

Unfurling my fingers, I gazed at the ring in my palm. Mythical beasts and Celtic designs decorated the ancient ring and danced in my eyes as light reflected off the large gemstone in the center. I just had to slip it on my finger and I'd launch through my visions to a new time and place, away from this prison of reform.

But my hand closed around the ring again. I couldn't leave Jayne. Her light was fading as her hope of getting her life back dwindled to a low ember. She needed my help.

My spine straightened as the clomp of hard shoes moved through the hall outside my door. Panic shot through me as I searched the room for a secure hiding place for the ring. I had to protect it with my life, knowing it had the power to save me.

The only place to conceal the ring was within the folds of the scratchy wool blanket on my cot. The sound of hard heels on the wood floor grew louder with each strike, causing my body to twitch.

What if they were going to move me now? The ring would be lost to me then. I had to keep it with me at all times.

The door knob rattled as a key pushed into the lock. My bones turned to ice, making my movements jerky as I shoved the ring into the waistband of my underwear. I stood up tall, straightening my frock to hide any evidence of my deviance, and waited as my heart pounded in my ears.

"Father Griffin has asked that the two of ye work off yer penance," Sister Francis' voice cut into the room. "Yer ta be moved from silent prayer to service." She opened the door wider and tapped her foot repeatedly. "Come on now."

Her hand waved at me in quick beats to get me moving as she grumbled under her breath something that sounded like, "He's no idea of the troubles from these two. He should trust my instincts and my methods..."

My eyes widened then in understanding.

Mother Maureen. She must have said something to the priest about our horrific treatment. Something that caused him to give new orders for our punishment.

A gift—a hidden opportunity for escape.

"What kind of service?" I asked, following her out of the room. We stopped in the hall, waiting, and a moment later Jayne joined us with another staff member.

My smile filled my entire face as I brightened just from seeing her. It was impossible to hide my relief that we were together again and I silently thanked Maureen for her genius scheming.

Jayne bounced to my side and we grabbed hold of each other's hands in elation. I stared into her eyes to let her know I had an idea.

A plan.

And she was a part of it.

"Not a word, you two. Service means work. And work it will be. Starting with the bathrooms." Sister Francis pushed us along the dreary hallway and we moved through the building as if heading to an elaborate gala. Cleaning bathrooms all day was paradise compared to the silence and loneliness of purgatory.

After brief instruction on our cleaning duties and a reminder of the strict expectation of silence, Sister Francis started us in the lower level bathroom used by the staff.

Multiple toilet stalls and showers filled the space, assuring me hours could be filled in there. Hours for planning and strategizing. But before my next thought could complete itself, Sister Francis found yet another way to control us.

"One at a time. Ya don't expect a social hour, I'm sure." She pointed to Jayne. "You. Out in the hall, while this one scrubs. Then, you'll change places. No talking or you'll be back in yer prayer rooms fer good." She ushered Jayne out into the corridor and positioned her by a faded portrait of the baby Jesus with a halo around his head. "Ten rounds on the rosary, then ye switch." She pressed the beads into Jayne's hand and then walked away into a room a few doors down.

Slopping a mop into a dirty bucket, I looked up and caught Jayne's eye. I glanced at her rosary beads, then back into her eyes and choked on a laugh. Her face fell at the thought of her predicament and then her mouth pressed together to stifle her chuckle. But it was too late. The laughter took us over and the more we tried to squash it, the worse it got.

Jayne's face turned beet red as she shook with silent laughter and bent over in muted guffaws. My legs crossed under me to keep from peeing myself in uncontrollable spasms of hushed laughter and then I remembered.

The ring.

I stood up straight and lifted my finger to my lips to silence Jayne. She froze and stared at me, waiting. I reached under my frock and grabbed hold of the ring, snug at my hip, and removed it from its hiding place. Holding the chain, careful not to touch the ring in any way that might set it into motion, I let the talisman hang and twirl in its weightless freedom.

The rosary beads slid from her fingers and hit the floor in a pile as she stared at the ring swaying from my hand.

"What is it?" she mouthed in silence.

I whispered back with clear certainty, "Our freedom."

CHAPTER 3

Jayne's eyes grew wide in response to the word freedom. At first, elation shone from her face, but then fear took its place. She'd been held at the reformatory for a lot longer than me, and judging by the shock in her expression, she likely hadn't expected a jailbreak any time soon.

Rustling from down the hall silenced us for longer than I could bear. My heels bounced in my shoes as I waited for the opportunity to tell her more.

Then, finally, it was my turn for repentance while Jayne scrubbed, and the change of guard opened fresh opportunity for more plotting.

"Jayne," I whispered to her while moving my fingers along the rosary to appear like I was praying out loud "My visions. You know how they call me a witch. I need to tell you more about it."

"Devil's bitch," she whispered back to me with a chuckle. "They'll burn you at the stake if you speak of it." Her eyes rolled up.

"Well, they're right. Sort of." I paused, searching for quick words that could explain the complexities of the situation. "I see things. It's called second sight. But it's more than that."

She stopped wiping the shower walls and listened harder.

"I can travel through my visions, Jayne. I know it sounds crazy. It's a curse really, but I think it could help us get out of here." I pressed on my frock where the ring hid. "And the ring helps make it happen."

The cleaning rag dropped from her hand as she stared at me, waiting for more information.

"We need to stage our disappearance." I mouthed most of my words.

"A drowning," Jayne stated. "Like a failed escape attempt."

My eyes shot wide. "Exactly!"

A loud clomp of heels on wood dropped my gaze onto my rosary.

"What do I hear? Whispering? Scheming?" The voice pierced my skin.

I continued moving my lips, whispering the Hail Mary under my breath as I lifted my gaze to Sister Francis. Our eyes met and I inched my fingers along the beads as if not wanting to be interrupted mid-prayer. She of all people should understand the disrespect of breaking one's movement through the rosary.

Holding her eyes without pausing my prayer, I didn't flinch under her aggressive accusation. I dropped my eyes back onto the beads and ignored her.

Her fury built as she clomped closer to me until she was standing right in front of my face. Her stale breath mixed with my air, violating my personal space.

"No dinner for you tonight." She huffed. "Yer too big for yer britches. Time ta size ya down a bit."

I didn't miss a beat on the rhythm of my repetition of prayer, infuriating her further. And no dinner tonight meant no laced juice. I'd learned quickly to stay away from that cocktail.

"Sure, ya'll work through the night as well. Father Griffin wanted service from ye. Service he'll get." And she stormed away with thunderous clomps.

I looked back to Jayne, who was rigorously scrubbing tiles to avoid any form of attack from Sister Francis.

"Yes. A drowning," I whispered. "Tonight. While everyone sleeps."

~

"I'm scared, Izzy." Jayne clamped onto my arm as we crept out the back door into the darkness of night.

We each carried an extra frock stolen from the laundry, and a second pair of shoes. We'd lay them on the beach, as if we'd gone for a swim. Once we were discovered missing, they would find the clothing and assume we'd made an attempt to swim to the mainland. A death sentence in and of itself.

"I know. Me too. If this works though, we'll be free from this place." I led her down toward the beach. "We can't just stay here and rot."

"But what will I do? Where will I live?" Her questions filled the air with worry.

"You'll stay with me until we figure all that out. But you can't stay here, Jayne. It's killing you. And it'll kill me too." I gripped her hand. "Do you understand?"

"Okay. Yes." Her eyes fell and she dropped her extra frock and shoes onto the sand. Then she looked at me with a new spark in her gaze. "This is gonna blow my mind, right? I hate you, you know. For doing this to me. Feckin' devil's bitch."

"Nothin' a harlot like you can't handle. Wench." I shoved her as I set my props in the sand haphazardly.

"They'll send me back, you know. If they find me." Jayne spoke into the open air.

"Yeah. Me too. No doubt about that." I looked back toward the quiet building. "But not without a fight."

"Damn straight."

"Hell, yeah." Then, following a strange, muffled sound—like a far off slamming door, my head shot to the side.

My hand rose to stop Jayne from making another sound and we listened.

"If it's that snitch, Theresa, again, I..."

"Shhh." I stifled Jayne and scanned the silent beach. "Okay, we better do this fast." I squeezed the ring in my hand. "So, we concentrate on sort of, umm..." My head shook. I'd never tried to do this under pressure. "I guess, if we both picture the same thing, like Doona Castle. Have you ever been there?"

"No." She shook her head.

"Okay. Shit. What about Rockfleet? Have you ever…" I stopped short as she cut me off.

"Yes! Field trip to Westport. I remember Rockfleet Castle," she yelped.

"Okay, perfect. Picture it. Every detail you can remember. I will too. And concentrate." I lifted the ring from my palm and studied it. "When I place this on my finger, hold on tight, and if it works, the wind will come and, okay, so, scary shit will happen. But it'll be okay. I promise."

"Nothing is scarier than Sister Francis' face. So get me the hell out of here. Even through your psycho-witch bullshit." She stared at the ring, nodding. "You're the best friend I ever had, Izzy." She looked me in the eye. "Now do it!"

I locked my elbow tighter with hers and shoved the ring onto my finger. In the exact same moment, forceful gusts battered us from every direction, whirling up all around.

"What's happening?" Jayne cried out.

"It's working. Stop pulling!" I shouted back.

My shoulders jolted from her tugging and I clamped onto her arm tighter.

"Izzy! Help me!" She screamed.

"Jayne!" I squinted through the blasting force of the wind, searching for her face. "Jayne, hang on!"

She continued to pull on me, causing me to stumble while the squall surged around us. I steadied myself and leaned in closer to help her navigate the forceful gusts.

"Let go of me," she yelled.

Her words shocked me but I held on tighter, pulling her closer to me.

"It will be okay, Jayne! I promise!" I shouted.

I caught glimpse of her in the tempest and stared into her terrified face. In an instant, I understood her beg for release wasn't meant for me. And just then, I reeled back from the unexpected sight of someone else's face.

Sister Francis and her twisted grimace filled my vision.

Her lips curled back, exposing gnashing teeth, and she ripped Jayne from me just as I was pulled into the whirling vortex.

Thunder pounded in my ears as blasts of stormy winds surged, pulling me from the beach, away from my prison. Images of Jayne's desperate eyes haunted me through the torrents and I reached through the chaos one last time in hopes of finding her hand.

All sound and fury concentrated around me to a point where it became near silence—a vacuum that held only a high pitch that hummed in the back of my mind. The void held me, suspended without any stimulation of my senses, and time lost its continuous measure. The high pitch grew like a sharp needle in my brain and pierced its way out of my skull into an explosion of blinding light and booming sound.

I reached for my head and squeezed with my forearms, holding it together before it shattered open. My teeth clenched tight as I rode the onslaught of the reawakening of my senses in a crashing force that shot my eyes open in terror.

Color streamed past me in a blur as tears tore from my eyes back into my hair. As I squinted and pressed my arms over my ears, a sound formed in my throat and escaped my mouth in a low moan that grew to a loud cry through clamped teeth.

Heavy shudders shook my body with turbulence and I realized I wouldn't survive such an assault. I was dying. My tears of fear turned to those of sorrow—sadness for not being able to complete the journey that I was just beginning to embrace.

And sadness for Jayne. I'd lost her and now would never be able to get back to her.

And then, smash! I landed as if from a great height with a wet splat that soaked my face and saturated every part of me. I remained motionless on the spongy ground and breathed in the fresh, composting scent of natural earth. Bog land. I took another breath, filling my lungs with the familiar smell of the Irish countryside.

I'd survived!

Elation surged through me as I squished my fingers into the wet ground. But then I gazed at the mud on my hands. There had been no bog land on the island of my captivity—only rock and sand. Had I really travelled to a new location?

My breath quickened with the hope of my escape from that wretched place and I blinked into the brightness of day like a newborn.

Jayne. She didn't make it. Sister Francis caught her and there was no telling what her punishment would be this time.

My eyes closed again in determination of getting back to Jayne. Rescuing her from that hell-hole.

And I would.

Planning how I would get back to Jayne brought vigor into my muscles and I pressed myself up to sitting. Stretching my arm muscles, I cracked my neck to each side. Then, pulling in one more enormous breath of oxygen, I widened my eyes as I scanned my surroundings.

My hands shot to the ground, bracing me at the sudden shock of my new setting. Looming in the distance, keeping formal watch over the open sea, dark stony walls climbed four stories high—Rockfleet Castle.

CHAPTER 4

It worked! The plan had worked.

I'd escaped from my hellish prison.

But without Jayne.

And I was in the wrong place.

I thought about the process that got me here, each step that brought the ring to me and then launched me off that wretched island.

My secret letter must have made its way to Maureen, showing her a rough sketch of the island and surrounding landscape. She and Ryan would have then been able to figure out my location.

All I had needed was the ring. That would be enough to set my freedom into motion and they knew it. Ryan was reluctant to even touch it, being all too aware of its power, but he still passed it along to Maureen and my escape plan began.

They had both come through for me and helped make my escape possible. And now my focus was to get back to them, to figure out what to do next.

But my vision had blasted me here to Rockfleet Castle. I was sure Ryan would be waiting for me at Doona Castle instead, but Jayne wasn't able to envision Doona in her mind. We'd pictured this location together when the vision started. So that would explain why I was in the wrong place.

Now I just had to find my way home. To Ryan.

Oh my god. I couldn't believe I was so close to seeing him again. My heart had ached for so long, it seemed like all it knew now. Tears stung my eyes and my throat tightened as I hoped our reunion would be everything I'd dreamed.

I scrunched my nose, trying to remember how far Doona Castle was from Rockfleet. Maybe thirty minutes by car.

My mind jumped to Jayne. I prayed she would stick to the plan, and after the force of the wind died down, she would search for me in the current. She'd drag Sister Francis along the coast as she screamed for my rescue from the swelling surf.

I pictured it in my mind—Jayne overdoing the theatrics of my drowning to take the focus off her own punishment for being outside when she should be scrubbing toilets all night. A small smile spread across my mouth as I thought of her wild antics. My harlot friend.

I vowed to rescue her.

I pressed on my knees and stood, wiping moss from my frock. The simple gray dress was all I had on and I was barefoot. Judging from the knots my fingers caught onto in my hair, I probably appeared like I'd just woken from winter hibernation.

I stumbled up a ravine, struggling to find my strength and balance, and watched Rockfleet come into full view.

In a panicked jolt, I crouched and then lay flat on my stomach to hide from view. The lone, brooding towerhouse of Rockfleet Castle was no longer a historical monument to Ireland's notorious pirate queen, but it was now alive and bustling with a village of activity surrounding it.

Outbuildings sent smoke into the air from their chimneys, while clanging sounds of pounding metal mixed with the scent of farm animals. Smaller huts with cone-shaped roofs and canvas walls surrounded the castle and their tapestry entryways flapped in the wind. The entire village appeared like a medieval fair preparing for its cosplay visitors.

My breath stopped as I scanned the activity around the castle. Something was wrong. Everything was different.

The asphalt roadway that had passed along the base of Rockfleet leading to the concrete docks was gone. Only a dirt path remained, leading to a port that had no sign of concrete but only wooden docks. And the most magnificent ship I'd ever seen, outside of pirate movies anyway. My eyes widened as my own gasp startled me.

Looking back toward the castle, I scanned the villagers going about their duties. Leather vests and pants, billowing blouses and hair tied back with cordage. The men appeared strong and determined. Women worked with the same focus as their skirts dragged through the mud and their shawls covered the multiple layers of heavy fabric of their garments.

I glanced down at the ring on my hand. The ring of Grace O'Malley, pirate queen. She was chieftain of the O'Malley Clan and Rockfleet was one of her strongholds. Maeve had told me all about it.

I froze in place as it all came crashing down on me.

The castle.

The village surrounding it.

The ship—it was her galley.

It was the time of Grace O'Malley. And this was her clan.

And it was very likely the point in time that Maeve had travelled to. And stayed in.

I shot my eyes back to the castle and fear welled up in my throat. Could Maeve be here? The thought terrified me. But it was everything I'd ever dreamed of—making contact with her. Knowing she was okay. And possibly bringing her back with me...if she would come.

I had to get inside.

It was my one chance to find Maeve.

To save her.

And ultimately, to save myself from the same fate.

Getting into the fortified castle without being discovered would be near impossible. Judging by the height of the sun in the sky, it was early morning, and the village bustled with chores for getting the day started.

My clothing alone would get me spotted from a mile away and the way things were in the past…it was lawless. Anything could happen to me. And I couldn't even be sure Maeve would be in there, if the timing was even right.

I cranked my mind through all the possible scenarios. No Maeve. Drawn swords. More accusations of being a witch. I glanced behind me, considering any possible exit, then gazed forward again and inched up to standing.

Maybe Grace would be there. I could speak with her about Maeve, and tell her things I knew of history, of her as a great leader. Then she might trust me.

I dropped my head back in disbelief at my own thoughts. They'd call me a witch for sure then. I'd be doomed.

With a huff, I hurried along the hilltop and traversed down beside a trickling brook. If I stayed among the boulders and hid against the sides of outbuildings, I could remain unseen for a bit longer. And then with my head down, looking determined, I might be able to walk right into Rockfleet like I belonged there.

I rolled my eyes at the naive simplicity of my plan, and then walked faster toward my destination.

I had no choice.

Once down the embankment, I ran to the back of the closest building. The pungent stink alone made it clear it housed livestock and then an early-morning chorus of neighing proved it held a great number of hungry horses too. I shimmied along the back of the barn, looking in all directions for any sign of a tipped-off clansman.

Moving around the rear corner, I crept along the wall to the front edge of the barn. I peered out across the settlement to search for my most direct, yet concealed, route to the castle. Its brooding black door beckoned me closer and I stared at the metal ring that offered entry in.

A cart with hay, a massive pile of stones, scaffolding half-built up the side of the castle wall—they all offered me shelter of some form.

I followed two men with my eyes as they spoke in deep tones that wove through the morning mist. Then a woman. Her skirts swept at the ground as she carried an armful of wood. Then there was a lull with no one around, and I dashed out from my hiding place.

At the cart of hay, I bent down and looked under it for any feet on the other side. With the coast clear, I darted around the mountain of stones and moved to the piles of wooden planks used to create scaffolding up the side of the castle.

Remaining still for a few moments to catch my breath and find my last bit of courage before moving around to the front of the castle, I squeezed my hand tight to feel the ring's presence. Its bulky weight assured me of its strong grip on my finger and gave me the final nudge to move ahead.

With small, quick steps, I glided along the stony side of the fortress, feeling mud oozing between my toes, and then stopped short.

"And where might you be goin' lassie? And in yer nightdress, no doubt?" The stern tone of a woman turned my head in a jerk.

With her arms full of wood, she held her head tipped in judgment, eyeing me.

Her eyebrows shot up. "Who are you? I've not seen ye here before." She glanced all around to be sure I didn't have any companions alongside.

"I'm...I'm lost," I started. "I've come to see Grace."

"Grace?" The wood in her arms wobbled.

Shit. Grace was her modern name. Maeve used to call her something else, something Gaelic. Gran-something. Gran-y-a-wail...something like that. Like, Grania, for short.

"Grania?" My weak voice squeaked out of me.

I lifted my eyes to meet hers, half-afraid she would call for help or send me away. But instead of meeting the eyes of a militant clanswoman, I looked into the bewildered face of a woman in shock.

Her pile of wood fell from her arms and rattled down onto the ground. I dodged back and she stepped at the same time, over the wood closer to me.

She studied me, up and down, and reached for my hair. I shrunk back from her touch but allowed her to examine me closer. Her fingers rubbed the fabric of my dress as her eyes moved across the details of its machine stitching.

Then she froze, staring at my hand. The ring.

She grabbed hold of my arm and, darting her eyes in both directions, she pulled me around to the front of Rockfleet Castle and right up to the door. Twisting the large metal knocker, she pulled the door open and shoved me inside. Slamming the door behind us, she took a huge inhale while staring at me, then let the air out of her lungs slowly.

"We've been waiting for you," she said.

A shiver ran up my spine. "What?"

"The curse. It's getting stronger. She's fading from us." She glanced up the ladder to the next level. "But now you are here. It is a miracle." She reached for me to come in further.

I followed her to a large fireplace that held a steaming cauldron. With a huge wooden spoon, she stirred the contents.

"Will ya have some porridge? Before I take you up?" she asked.

I followed her line of vision along the wooden ladder to the next level.

She intended to take me up there. But to who? Grace? Was she sick? Dying, maybe?

"No, thank you," I said, looking up the rickety ladder. "I'm ready to go up there now."

CHAPTER 5

The clanswoman dropped the wooden spoon into the porridge and watched me with a knowing eye, like she'd met me before or knew I'd be coming. And I had to admit, there was something familiar about her as well. Like a distant aunt or someone from a dream. But it was the desperation in her eyes that bothered me most. Something was wrong and she looked to me like I held the power to make it right.

She sent me up the ladder first and followed at my heels. Pushing myself up the last few wobbling rungs, I stepped onto the second floor and scanned the food storage and makeshift sleeping quarters. She ushered me up the next ladder, which was in better repair and likely less frequently used.

I climbed again, wobbling on the leather-tied steps, praying it wouldn't come away from the wall and drop me backwards. Her close proximity to my feet kept me moving quickly and I crawled onto the next floor with clumsy technique. Pushing up to standing, I stared at full sets of armor, piles of leather outerwear, and shields and swords. A complete armory filled my vision and my heart pounded in my chest.

I turned back to her, my mouth hanging open, speechless.

"Now, you take the spiral stairs there. Up to her chambers. I'll be waitin' down below if'n ya need for anythin'. Just call fer me. Maggie," she said.

"Maggie?" I repeated.

"Yes, dear. And yer name be?"

"I'm Isobel Ross. Pleased to meet you." I nodded.

"Ach, yeh've grown, lassie, into a strong, young woman." She winked.

"Do I know you?" I asked.

"Ah, sure. 'Twas long ago. Go on now." She nudged her head at the spiral stairs and turned to the ladder. "Up ya go." Without a second thought, she moved down the rungs with ease.

I stared at the space where she had stood. Who was she? Maggie? I pressed my eyes shut, trying to remember her, but couldn't make any connections.

Then I turned to the spiral staircase and moved my eyes up along its curves.

Taking a deep breath, I climbed each awkward step, some steeper than others, all curling in an unnatural direction. Keeping my hand along the outer wall for stability, I moved up the cold, stone stairs.

At the top, I froze for a moment and held my breath. I was about to enter the private chambers of Grace O'Malley, clan chieftain of the sixteenth century, and my heart rate quadrupled.

I took a step forward and entered the impressive space. I threw my gaze around the room and in the middle, surrounded by tapestries, an enormous fireplace, treasure chests, and animal fur rugs, was a four-post bed.

A strong man sat on the edge of the bed holding the woman's hand with gentle care. His massive shoulders slumped as she lay motionless under his worried watch.

I stepped closer and his head shot up in response to the sound of my movement. He stood in an instant, facing me, and his broad stature filled the room.

"What have ye?" he asked.

I stared at him, having no idea what he was asking. I froze, speechless.

"Have ye word?" He stepped closer as his voice grew louder.

Stepping back from his intimidating advance, I spat whatever words found their way into my mouth.

"I've come to help," I said. "I might be able to help." I tipped my head to look past him, toward the bed. "Can I see her?"

His eyes narrowed as he studied me. Then, trusting that Maggie had sent me up, he stepped aside, gesturing toward her.

"Thank you," I said as I stepped past him closer to the bed. Once my eyes went beyond his tall, protective stature, I saw her.

Long brown hair with several small braids throughout. Face of an angel. Or one of a warrior princess.

My breath sucked in and I gasped. My hand flew to my mouth but only after her name shot from my lips.

"Maeve!"

~

"The Druids. They've placed a curse on her, ya see." He paced by the fireplace as I continued to hold her hand. "They think she's a witch. Carrying with her prophecies of things to come."

I gazed into Maeve's face. Her closed eyes fluttered and she squeezed my hand with what little strength she had. I couldn't be sure if she knew it was me, but something in my soul said she did.

"Why? I don't understand," I asked him through clenched teeth.

"They are a holy order, moving with the rhythms of the earth. When Maibh came, they felt a disruption." He threw a small rag into the fireplace. "They've blamed all ill happenings on her. They think..." He hesitated as his words caught in his throat. "Ya see, they believe her prophecies. And want to stop her predictions from coming true. Stopping her, they believe, will stop the apocalypse as they know it." He looked into my eyes. "Stopping time is what they want."

Stopping time? I looked at the ring on my hand again. It held the power of time, he was right. And somehow, between Maeve and me, we harnessed that power.

I thought back to his words and the way he said her name, Maibh. It was magical. Lyrical. The weight of his words and the sadness in his tone proved his love for her. Deep worry lines in his face showed significant passage of time with Maeve in this condition, worsening.

I moved my fingers along Maeve's forehead and down her cheek. "Maeve, I'm here. It's Izzy. I'm going to help you," I said.

I had no idea how I could help her, but she needed me.

Her hand tightened around mine.

"I feel your grip, Maeve. I know you are strong," I whispered to her. Then, turning to her steadfast watchman, I pleaded, "Why are they doing this to her?"

"To preserve Gaelic Ireland. To save it from the obliteration Maibh has prophesized," he said. "Protecting it from the Brits. From the new world." He kicked soot back into the fireplace. "They intend to influence time and they believe Maibh to be the gatekeeper. If they can stop her, they can stop the progression of time. Then their power will be boundless."

"How do we stop this curse?" I blasted at him.

"No one knows. Only the Druids understand their magic." He stepped to the window and gazed out. "They've lined it up in accordance with the seasons. Maibh gets worse with each passing equinox. It's only with the solstice that she breathes and shines the light of hope from her eyes. But soon, I fear there will be nothing left of her."

I stood up from her bed and stormed over to him. "We can't just let her die!" My loud voice shook. "We need to bring the Druids back. To reverse whatever they've done to her," I demanded.

He glared at me through narrowed eyes. After a moment, he said, "This plundering group of Druids, they are nomads. A rogue society with their own ideology. Hooligans. Scattered to the wind." He moved to the window and glanced out. "I have my scouts, as well as the honorable Druids, searching for them every day. Yet nothing." His voice trailed off in distraught frustration.

I lifted my hand to my forehead and pushed my fingers into my hair. How could I help her if I had no idea about the mystical ways of the Druids? I didn't even know what the force was that was draining her life energy. I closed my eyes in thought and—bam!

He grabbed onto my wrist and my eyes shot open. He pulled my hand away from my hair and held it firmly in his grasp.

I gasped from the sudden aggressive contact and the powerful strength of his hold. Something turned in him and his eyes bored into mine. Did he think I was here to harm her?

"What is this?" His voice pierced through my soul. "You are the messenger? The one we've been waiting for?"

"What?" I pulled my wrist back with little success.

He turned my arm and pushed the back of my hand up to my face. Staring back at me from my middle finger was the ring.

The ring of the pirate queen.

"Yeh've her ring!" he blasted. "Where did you get it? We thought it to be lost forever, having disappeared into the mist of time." His eyes widened with dread as if he were seeing something that shouldn't be seen. It was terror of centuries colliding but his unmistakable awe also held the power of hope.

With my other hand, I pulled my wrist to my heart and held the ring there. "Yes," I gasped, then looked to Maeve. "It's her ring. It's been protected through generations, waiting for this moment."

I turned back to him as our faces lit up and he nodded.

"Yeh must return it to her," he said. "She's been fading without it, like a part of her soul was lost, or set in limbo, when it disappeared."

We inched closer to Maeve and stared into her face.

I pulled the ring from my finger and rolled it in my palm.

He was right. The ring was Maeve's connection to this time. Without it, she was trapped in a suspended state, powerless.

Maybe the ring could help her now. His fixed stare and shallow breathing proved he believed it too.

Lifting Maeve's hand from her fur blanket, I pushed the ring onto her finger.

In the jolt of a life saving gasp, she inhaled as if resuscitating from drowning. Her eyes shot wide open and she sat straight up, staring into my soul.

My hair blew back from my face and I smiled at Maeve. As if no time had passed, we gazed at each other like long lost sisters who'd been reunited after an eternity of separation.

The wind whipped my hair into my eyes and I lost sight of her. I swatted at it, desperate to see her face again. But then my senses pulled into a vacuum of nothingness as I ripped away from her.

I launched into the abyss of my visions.

CHAPTER 6

Every sound in the universe collided into a mind-shattering drone of chaos as I blasted through a spiraling vortex. All of my senses were exploding, like being trapped at the epicenter of the Big Bang. Bright light blinded me and I was deafened from the intensity of the expanding surge of continuous thunder. Every nerve shook and I tightened my muscles to keep from bursting into a million pieces, scattering throughout the cosmos.

Then, crash!

I hit with a jolt.

Pressing up onto my bruised elbows, I shivered with cold that penetrated my bones as I blinked into a wall of darkness.

Light shone above me through a narrow opening and I pulled myself through the damp passageway toward the glow. I'd landed on solid rock and my rattled bones ached from the impact but the spine-chilling, cavernous darkness behind me kept me moving.

The sound of my wriggling echoed deep within the space in the earth and my hair stood on end at the thought of the unearthly creatures that might lurk in its depths, ready to pull me back down into their lair.

As I struggled closer to the light, my hands rustled through twigs and dry leaves and I kept my eye on the opening between large rocks that offered my escape. I reached for the edge of one of the boulders and pulled myself out into the fresh, misty air. A salty breeze brushed across my face, welcoming me with its familiar scent.

Blinking into the bright light of day, my eyes adjusted and pulled in an overload of sensory information. In an instant, I called out.

"Ryan!" His name stuck in my parched throat.

He sat at the edge of the clearing at Doona across from me, shoulders slumped, staring out to sea.

I coughed and called out again. "Ryan!"

His head shot up.

"Isobel!" he cried out, and ran to me. "Isobel. Jesus Christ!" He dropped to his knees and reached around my shoulders, pulling me into his chest. "Oh my god. Are you hurt?"

Every muscle and every bone in my body cried out in pain, but the joy of being held in his arms dulled it and I reached around him, pulling myself into him.

In that same moment, my mind filled with every thought and emotion in his being. Our contact opened a channel between us and I knew he saw everything I'd been through too.

The sorrow in his heart for not being able to get me out of the institution sooner tore at him—weakened him. But there was something more. Something else sapping his energy, like his gift was fading. But my focus hovered on his raw love for me as it burst my heart open.

"I can't believe you're here. Jesus. You've been through hell." His body shook as he released me and shimmied back. "Best we don't touch for too long. I don't want to chance anything else happening." He swallowed hard. "I just want you here with me. To stay."

I reluctantly released him, knowing it was dangerous to touch, just in case it might invoke another vision. I didn't have the strength to do that again. And plus, the contact of our reunion seemed to drain him and he slouched now.

But being with Ryan…nothing else mattered. I gazed into his eyes, holding our intense connection without touch.

"I was at Rockfleet. Did you see it all?" I inched closer to him to get his scent and to pick up on the heat that radiated from him.

He moved his face closer to mine, examining my features. "I saw everything. Maeve. Rockfleet. Sister Francis. Jayne."

I gasped. "Jayne! I need to go back for her!"

"I know. We will. I just need to get you home, safe, cleaned up. You've been through too much." His face twisted in pain.

"I'm okay." My voice shook. "There's just so much..." My thoughts snarled into themselves as I pieced everything together.

There was a curse.

It kept repeating through my mind. A curse that nearly ended Maeve. And it intended to end us all. To stop the progression of time.

Maybe returning the ring to Maeve had been the catalyst to end the curse, but the deep pit in my stomach proved otherwise. It felt more like a bad omen that foretold this wasn't the end, but just the beginning.

I looked back at the crevice between the boulders where I had pulled myself out of the deep cavern. Dried stems and ribbons trailed out of the space where I'd dragged my battered body from the darkness. It was the space where Paul had been leaving flowers for Maeve, for years. The hoard had piled up to an unmeasurable amount of visits and longing.

But the space between the rocks went further than I'd realized before.

Deeper. Much deeper.

It was a passageway.

A gateway that drew my fascination toward its darkest depths. It lured me with its mystery and intrigue.

Following close behind Ryan, I stumbled along the trail heading down from the clearing and looked back toward the mysterious, secret cavern.

"It leads to something," I mumbled.

"Hmm?" Ryan reached for me to be sure I was stable.

"Between the boulders. There's a passageway. I think it leads to something big. The echoes went deep." My words trailed off as his truck came into view.

Parked by the ancient cemetery just beyond Doona Castle, the sight of Ryan's truck elated me as I filled my lungs with a huge breath of joy. Modern technology. A connection to home. I smiled from deep within my heart.

"I need to get you to Eileen, straight away, before word gets to her from the institution." Ryan planned out loud.

He was right. Gram needed to know I was okay. If word got to her of my drowning, it could be devastating to her health. She'd likely have a stroke or some form of collapse. We had to get to her first.

But then, after that, I intended to go back to the clearing to explore the underground cave.

"Does she know about Mother Maureen's jailbreak?" I smirked.

"No. We didn't mention it in case it didn't work." He reached in his pocket to check for his keys. "We've been trying to protect Eileen as best we can. She's quite fragile since you were sent away. Her not knowing of your well-being, it's been torture for her. Like you were sent to prison and they threw away the key." His steps grew heavier and pounded in the dirt.

"How could they do that to me?" My teeth clenched. "How was it even legal?"

"They said you were a threat to yourself and others. That you had to be rehabilitated. Sanctioned. That's all I was told." He picked up a stone and hurled it toward the sea. "Someone needs to pay. Someone needs to take responsibility for it." His words choked out of him.

His anger was palpable and filled the space around us. I just wanted to hold him again. To feel his heart beat in his chest and the warmth of his touch.

"We'll figure it out. Together. We just have to be sure nothing pulls us apart again. Please." Fear crept into my voice.

I had to do everything in my power to avoid being arrested and sent away again. Without the ring, now that it was back with Maeve, I wouldn't have a chance at escaping a second time.

"I gave the ring to Maeve. To save her life," I said.

"I know. I felt it." He opened the passenger side of the truck and I climbed in.

I looked back at him. "What do you mean, you felt it?"

He cracked open a water bottle and passed it to me. "Drink." He watched me take a sip. "Something shifted in me when you passed the ring to her. I felt strong again, like my senses were still at full strength, but only for a short time." A plane flew overhead and our eyes followed it. "The curse of the Druids. I saw it when I held you and you're wondering if it's over now."

"It could be," I interjected. "Maybe returning the ring had the power to stop it. Like, reconnecting the past with the present."

He shook his head. "It's not over. Not by a long shot. It makes sense to me now. It's causing things to fade, like the power of the seers, weakening. These things are starting to disappear. Like we..." He paused. "Like *we* might disappear."

My hand jolted and water splashed onto my knee. "That's what her guardian said," I interjected. "The man who kept watch over her. He said *she* was fading, like she would disappear." I looked into Ryan's eyes, searching for his light, which appeared dimmer. "I thought giving her the ring would stop it. Like, open up time again for her, giving her the strength to remain where she was or to come home. And end the curse."

He motioned for me to drink more. "I don't know. We noticed our abilities becoming weaker while you were gone. You should have seen Maureen's frustration when her sight became clouded."

My breath sucked in. If our gifts ceased to exist, then everything would end. The hope of stopping the curse relied on our gifts, and without them, we'd have no hope.

"I feel it, too," I admitted. "It's different." I took a deep drink. "I couldn't conjure a vision while I was on the island. I figured it was the meds." I looked back toward the clearing. "But now I realize. Something's wrong."

"Other things too," Ryan mumbled.

"What other things?"

His gaze turned out the window and scanned the horizon. "I'm not sure. Strange things…changing." His voice trailed off as he gazed at the landscape. "Let me get you home. We can talk more once you're rested. Right now, I just want to look at you. And have you with me."

I melted into the safety of my seat, pushing aside all my questions. They could wait. Instead, I savored the time with Ryan in the sanctuary of his truck.

As he pulled the truck out from its spot behind the cemetery, a waft of stale air passed over my face, carrying with it the foul stench of decay. Echoes from the cavern replayed in my mind and I envisioned the depths filled with the reek of hell's rotten breath.

But then, tin whistles and drums laced the breeze. And a voice, lost in the wind. Calling to me in the darkest recess of my mind.

It cried out to me. Over and over. Pulling my attention back up the hills to the clearing.

The passageway.

I had landed in its narrow entry after my return from Rockfleet. At the time, getting out was my primary focus. But now…

It screamed for me and I could think of nothing else.

Curled up in my seat, I faded in and out of sleep while keeping my half-gaze on Ryan as we drove home to Galway. My tired eyes trailed through his hair and along his square jawline as I imagined him holding me.

He felt my desire on him and smiled, glancing over at me any chance he got.

"Yer trouble. You know that, right?" He chuckled.

I grinned and struggled to keep my eyes open, not wanting to miss a moment of him.

"We're here," he whispered, popping my eyes open in surprise.

I'd fallen asleep for the rest of the trip and nearly kicked myself for losing even a second of being with him.

I gazed out my window. "Where are we?"

"Behind Hilltop. The truck will blend in with the other deliveries to the shop. Put this on." He pulled a sweatshirt from the back of the cab and handed it to me. "Pull the hood onto your head for cover." He lifted his own hood up too. "Let's go."

Keeping our heads down, we walked at a quick pace along Dr. Mannix Road toward Gram's. Checking for any oncoming cars or passersby, we darted into her driveway and pushed through the gate leading along the side of the house to the back door. Ryan pressed me against the back wall of the house for cover and knocked gently on the door.

The sound of a chair scraping along the floor vibrated out to me and I pictured Gram standing from the table where she was probably having her cup of tea. Her voice travelled through the walls as she caught a glimpse of Ryan out the window.

"Ryan, dear." She shuffled to the door and pulled it open. "Ryan, come in. What are you doing back here?"

He looked into her frail face. "Eileen. I've news."

Her gasp could be heard for miles and I couldn't hide from her any longer. I stepped out from the shadows and pulled my hood down.

"Oh my Jesus. Tanks be ta God." She smacked her hand to her mouth then nearly fell out of the house to embrace me. "My beautiful Isobel." Her sobs stifled her voice as she held me.

"She's escaped from the institution," Ryan explained. "They likely think she drowned so I expect they'll be delivering the bad news to you shortly. You'll need to play along, Eileen. For Isobel's sake. To keep her safe from them."

"How can I ever thank you, Ryan?" Gram sobbed and squeezed me tighter. "Yer an angel from above."

"Nah, sure, Isobel orchestrated it. Maureen played a part as well. Once she got the cryptic letter from Isobel, we devised the plan to get to the island." Ryan pulled his hood forward, concealing more of his face.

Gram narrowed her eyes. "Somethin' tells me you had more than a hand in it. You're a thinker, lad." She tapped on the side of her forehead.

I darted my eyes to Ryan. He was behind the entire plan. Disguising Maureen as a nun. Getting her onto the ferry to the island. How did I miss it?

He pulled his hoodie further around his face as if to avoid too much attention and gave a subtle nod.

I glared at him for withholding that information and craved him even more because of it.

Gram soaked me in through her misted eyes. "You've received your diploma, sweetheart." She smiled. "Dr. McGratt submitted a summary of yer field work, sure, they attached an award of recognition to it." She sniffled.

My back straightened. I hadn't thought about school for even a moment, but now that I knew it was done, it released a clamp of anxiety that had lodged permanently in my chest.

"She can't stay here, Eileen. It's too risky," Ryan said. "I need ta bring her to Maureen so we can make a plan. We'll hide her for a bit while we decide what to do next. Okay?" He lifted his eyes and waited for her to process the request.

Gram looked into my face and nodded. "Okay."

Ryan walked toward the side of the house and gestured for me to follow. "We need to keep moving. I'm sorry. You'll have to say goodbye. For now."

Gram and I embraced and she held my face in her hands. "You will do great things, Isobel Ross. You have a purpose and now is your time."

Tingles shot through my spine as her words widened my eyes. She believed in me. She finally understood my journey was unique and necessary.

Ryan and I moved quickly along the side of the house and out onto the sidewalk. I turned back for one more glimpse of my home, not sure when I would see it again.

As I faced forward, I watched a car slow and pull along the side of the road just in front of us. The driver glanced at each house along the street, likely checking for numbers. My eyes jumped to the passenger in the car and landed on a familiar scowl that took a bead on Ryan.

"Shit!" I whispered in panic. "Don't look up. Keep walking," I commanded Ryan as I tucked my face further into my hood.

My heart rate accelerated to flight mode and my feet quickened their pace toward Ryan's truck. Keeping my head down, I prayed she hadn't seen me. And now I knew for sure, she was on her way to my house to tell Gram the news of my demise.

Ryan kept a cool strut to not raise suspicion and moved his arms as if lost in animated conversation. "Who the hell is it?" he murmured from the side of his mouth.

I glimpsed back only to see the car still stopped in the same location.

"Sister Goddamn Francis," I choked, and sped my pace to near running.

CHAPTER 7

"Do you think she saw you?" His panicked tone filled the truck's cabin and quaked my bones.

If Sister Francis had seen me, we wouldn't have made it to the truck. She wasn't the type to lose a fight and for some reason, this one seemed to be the prized fight of her lifetime.

She had likely obsessed, every waking moment, on ways to make my life miserable at the institution and there would be no stopping her now. Even believing I was in the afterworld, she had to be the one to bring the unfortunate news to Gram. My teeth ground at the thought of her finding some sick form of amusement in watching Gram fall apart.

"No. I don't think she knew it was me. She wouldn't expect it, thinking I was dead." I shook my hands to get the jitters out and grabbed my water bottle. "Thank god we got to Gram before her." I turned back to be sure we weren't followed.

Ryan pulled the truck out of Hilltop's lot and drove in the opposite direction of Sister Francis, taking the long way to the Spiddal road.

"They don't seem to waste any time delivering bad news." Ryan glanced at me through narrowed eyes. "Maureen'll be glad to see you. Let's hope she and that Sister Francis never meet." He chuffed. "She's been anxious these days. The locals have backed off a bit, relieving some of the pressure of driving us out. You know, now that the land is a historical site. Hands off. But still..."

I sat up taller now that we were far from Sister Francis' scowl. Hearing of Maureen was what mattered now.

He swerved to miss a sheep standing at the edge of the road. "I think, once you were sent away, they all felt a sick sense of accomplishment for having some form of consolation prize. You know, the witch hunters." He gripped the wheel until his knuckles went white.

"The church ladies, and the county council, they shouldn't have that kind of power." I squeezed my empty water bottle, crushing it in my hand. "They're ruining lives at the institution. None of those girls are criminals. They don't deserve to be treated that way. Such simple-minded thinking." I huffed. "I gotta get Jayne out of there, if it's the last thing I do."

"Well, let's see what Maureen has to say. She'll know what to do next." He glanced at me from the corner of his eyes, as if measuring what I might do.

And I knew well the next thing I needed to do. There was no doubt in my mind. I had to go back to the clearing. It had called to me for years, and I'd find myself there, again and again, searching for answers.

But this time, it was shouting to me.

Commanding for my return.

The sounds that filled my mind from deep within the subterranean passage generated patterns behind my eyelids. Ancient Celtic shapes that remained as shadows each time I blinked.

My mind could focus on nothing else but its demand for my return—to the hidden passageway between the boulders.

It had always been there. I'd visited the site more times than I could count, never knowing its hidden secret.

I just hadn't been ready to find it.

But now, it was time. To investigate.

I was ready.

~

Maureen barreled out of the cottage, tripping over herself, as we pulled into the yard.

"Jazus, Mary, and Joseph," she cried out, blessing herself. "Pull into the back." She swung her arms, directing Ryan out of sight, and followed the truck to the concealed backyard.

Before I could even hop out, her arms wrapped around me.

"Ach, you're a sight for sore eyes." She pulled back and had a good look at me. "Seein' ya trapped on that island broke me soul. But ya got yerself out. I'm proud of you." She hugged me again.

"Come on, Shanny. Let 'er into the house before any nosy neighbors get a whiff of the ungodly carry-on here at O'Shaughnessy's." He shot his eyebrows high.

"Sure, yer right, lad." She ushered me in after him through the back door.

Within seconds, the kettle was boiled and cups of tea covered the table. My shoulders relaxed from their high position around my ears and I gazed at the vintage trinkets all around the quaint cottage. My eyes landed on the smoldering coal fire that filled the space with warmth and welcome.

"Even in June, we like ta have a fire here," Maureen said. "It keeps the damp out of the old cottage. Keeps the thatch fresh and dry, too." She spoke into the glow of the embers.

My head shot back to her and Ryan. "June?" My breath stopped.

They stared back at me in silence.

"What do you mean, June?" My eyes widened. "What's today's date?"

"'Tis June 10th, Isobel." Maureen studied me.

I dropped my cup down onto the table, spilling some tea. "But it was only the middle of April when I was sent away. How could it already be June?" I counted the weeks on my fingers. "Six weeks? Eight?"

They continued to stare, speechless, then Ryan finally spoke. "How long did you think you were there?" He tipped his head.

I exhaled, looking down at my hands in my lap, trying to calculate how long I'd been gone.

"I don't know. Two weeks, maybe. Three?" I huffed. "I don't...I mean, they had me drugged most of the time. Everything was a fog."

Ryan's fist slammed down on the table and he stood. His chair fell behind him and smashed to the ground. Maureen jumped, sloshing her tea out of her cup and onto the table.

"They'll fuckin' pay fer that! Takin' you prisoner with no fair trial. It was a set up. A fuckin' 21st century witch hunt," he shouted.

"Settle down, Ryan," Maureen moved her hand in gentle waves. "That won't help anyone right now. We're all dissatisfied with the workins of the system."

"Dissatisfied?" he blasted. "I'm fuckin' pissed to the point of irrational." He dropped his head back and pushed his hands through his hair.

I smiled a little, watching his rant. His fury on my behalf was actually sexy beyond belief.

"The best revenge will be to expose them," I said. "To stop their control over other people's lives." I smirked a sinister grin. "And I aim to get it done sooner than later."

Ryan picked his tipped chair up from the floor and sat in it again.

A mortar and pestle had bounced to the edge of its shelf from the banging. I reached for it and placed it on the table. Remnants of herbs and seeds nestled at the bottom of the mortar and I stirred them with the pestle.

I prepared myself to tell Maureen about my visit to Rockfleet. The details would sound crazy, but if anyone was to believe it, it would be Maureen. And of course, Ryan. So I was in good company.

"When I put the ring on..." I paused and watched Maureen scoot closer. "It started my vision. You know, it worked."

Ryan nodded and I continued.

"It didn't just transport me to the clearing though. It took me somewhere else first. To Rockfleet Castle."

"Out past Westport?" Maureen asked.

"Yes. But it was different. It was a different time." I hesitated, not knowing what she was ready to hear.

"Yes, I know about that. Ryan's told me of your experiences, you know, of the visions." She stumbled on her words.

I looked at Ryan and he bent his head toward Maureen, encouraging me to go on.

I took a deep breath and told Maureen every detail of my visit to Rockfleet. From finding Maeve as she was losing her battle to the Druid's curse, and then passing the ring to her for strength, but leaving it behind.

She sat back in her chair as the final parts of the story finished. Rubbing her hands together, she closed her eyes in thought. I peeked over at Ryan, wondering what was going to happen next and he tapped his fingers on the table, not knowing. Then she spoke.

"I've felt it. Recently, too." She pulled the mortar and pestle toward herself and stirred the mysterious contents.

"What do you mean?" I asked.

Ryan repositioned himself in his seat.

"The Druid's curse. It's all around us now," she stated, staring into the mortar as if reading it. "My sight has become clouded. But then there's more." She pounded the pestle and looked at Ryan.

My eyes darted between the two of them.

Ryan chimed in. "We've noticed a pattern of unexplainable disruptions." He hesitated. "In modern technology."

"Like what?" I asked.

"Cell phones. Computers. Connectivity, in general. The glitches in service are causing mayhem through the country. No one can explain it."

"But then," Maureen interjected, "we noticed the absence of things that we had taken for granted over the years. It's as if they never existed." She paused. "Modern amenities that never were. You may not even remember them."

I studied Maureen's kitchen, looking for evidence of what she was saying, but my mind drew a blank.

"We think it's the start of a process," Ryan added. "Regression. Time moving backward."

"So the curse is working," I stated.

Maureen nodded. "And it just might have the power to finish us."

~

The hairs on my arms bristled from her harrowing words. Maureen felt the curse of the Druids. She said it was all around us.

Maureen pounded the pestle into the herbs. "I've seen your light dimming, Ryan. I wasn't sure why or how. I thought it was for worrying and missing Isobel. But now, it's all coming together. I know it's more than that."

My heart quickened. I had noticed the same thing with Ryan when we were first reunited at the clearing.

She continued, "If the Druid's curse carries on, it will ultimately succeed in its purpose. And its purpose is as old as Ireland herself." She scanned the antique trinkets on her shelves. "The Druids exist to preserve Gaelic Ireland. It is the path of Druidry." She dropped the pestle with a bang. "And controlling nature, understanding the rhythm of the seasons. It's what they do. And so, even the curse of a rogue clan of Druids can permeate everything around us. Every echo. Every vibration."

"That can't be possible," I blurted. "The curse was from five hundred years ago."

"Oh, Isobel. But it is. The power of the Druids is connected to everything around us. Even what we cannot see. The Druids are in the air we breathe and the ground we walk on. They are of time itself."

She stood and lifted the mortar of ground herbs from the table. Walking across the room, she approached the fire and threw the contents onto the coals. Sizzling and snapping, sparks shot around the embers and flecks of glowing herbs brightened the hearth.

Maureen turned back to us. "Whatever the curse may be, it's draining the essence of our gifts."

I jumped to my feet. "It's definitely why I couldn't conjure a vision at the institution. I know now it wasn't the meds, because even in my moments of clarity, a vision never came. Not until I had the power of the ring with me."

The last words caught in my mouth and choked me. I needed to get the ring back if we were going to attempt to break the curse that plagued Maeve's world and now seeped into ours. A curse that was draining the magic from our lives—what made us who we were.

I stared at Ryan, wondering how something so old could still have an effect on us. "So maybe my visions could take me back to Maeve, to truly break the curse at its point of origin."

He smacked his hand on the table. "Jesus Christ!" He exhaled loudly through his nose. "There's too much unknown. Ya could get lost again." He hesitated. "And, hell, we don't know if you could even get a vision to start."

Maureen gazed at me. "If you did go back, you would face the Druids."

Blood drained from my head at the thought of confronting the Druids. I'd heard about them in mythology and legends my entire life. I'd imagined them to be a nomadic tribe of wise, holy men, maintaining the order of ancient Ireland through mystical rituals.

"But it seemed like I already ended the curse. When I put the ring on Maeve's finger." I shook my head in frustration as I recalled her life-saving gasp, her rejuvenation. "I just can't believe that wasn't enough."

"It was a start, I s'pose. But there's no tellin' what happened after you left Rockfleet. And now, without the ring, I'm not sure what more can be done." Maureen stared into the dying fire.

"Then I must get the ring back now." I stood and paced around the table.

"But how?" Ryan cut my words short. "You're just back…" His words trailed off.

He wasn't ready to lose me again, and honestly, neither was I. The risk of getting trapped or lost in the vortex of time was always at the back of my mind and creeping to the forefront with every new sentence of our conversation.

We needed more information. It wasn't safe to just run blind.

"A visit to Paul, for starters," I stated. "He'll have knowledge of historical events from that time and maybe even some information on the Druids. We need his help."

Ryan pushed away from the table and launched up. He moved toward the front door and surveyed the yard as if searching for spies. "It's too dangerous. We need to keep you hidden."

He pressed the door open and took a first step out onto the stoop, as if needing fresh air. Within two seconds, he stumbled back in smashing into the door frame with a jerk.

Maureen jumped from the sudden motion and dropped the mortar from her hands. It smashed down and broke into pieces on the floor.

Ryan jolted toward the explosive sound, exposing his panicked eyes.

"Hide, Isobel! Quick!" he commanded me. "It's Mrs. Flannery."

CHAPTER 8

Shit! What the hell was Mrs. Flannery doing here? I stumbled over myself, flying to the back of the cottage. There was no way word could have travelled to her that fast.

But she was here to gloat, no doubt about it. To somehow feign her condolences only to watch Maureen and Ryan suffer under her judgmental glare.

My stomach squirmed as I ran to Ryan's room and slammed the door behind me.

Mrs. Flannery's shrill voice pierced through Ryan and Maureen's blockade at the front door and curled my toes with its vile intrusion. Steady mumbles quickly turned to short commands of "Good day. Be off with you now," from Maureen. She wasn't having any of Mrs. Flannery's fake social graces today.

My bones rattled as I cowered on Ryan's bed, pulling the duvet up around my chin. Nosy neighbors were the last thing we needed right now, particularly the one who put the final steps of my horrific incarceration into motion. I chewed on my cuticles, waiting for Ryan.

After a good slam of the front door—a direct communication from Maureen—Ryan crept into his room on tip-toes.

"She's gone," he whispered. "What a bitch."

I sat up straight, propped into the far corner of his bed. "What'd she want?"

"What we suspected." He turned back toward her direction. "She got the news from Sister Margaret. Was probably looking forward to delivering it to us." He pressed his back against the door, closing it behind him. "Maureen and I didn't flinch at the story of your disappearance. You should've seen the disappointment on her face. It was vile."

I huffed. "Just as well. She doesn't deserve the satisfaction." I dropped the duvet from my chin and scooted closer to the middle of the bed. "You'd think she'd be over this by now, thinking she'd ruined us. It's crazy she's still not content."

"A bitter woman," he said. "Needs to mess with people's happiness since she never had any of her own."

He stepped closer to the bed and sat on the edge. The dark circles under his eyes made him look like he hadn't slept in weeks. Maybe he hadn't. Eight weeks, to be exact…apparently. His exhaustion deepened his eyes, making them an abyss of dark blue, and his messy hair brought a smile to my face.

"What?" he asked.

"You look cute." I smirked.

"Shit." He ran his hand through his hair. "That's what I feel like."

I crawled over to him and brought my face right up to his. "I can make you feel better." I smiled into his eyes.

His eyebrows lifted and his hands moved as if they would touch me. "Don't. Please. It's too risky." He inched away. "I feel like I just got you back. I don't want anything else to happen right now." His hands hovered near me.

I inched closer. "Screw that. We've touched before without a vision starting. I want to. Just for a minute. Please," I begged.

His breathing accelerated with his draining resistance.

I inched closer and licked my bottom lip.

His hands landed on me in an instant. Holding my face, running through my hair. He reached around my back and pulled me into him.

"Jesus," he whimpered, holding me tighter. "Yer wicked thoughts are enough to kill me."

He hovered at my face, lingering just out of reach and his breath on my lips started a frenzy within me. I reached around his neck, pulling him in, and kissed him.

An explosion of our emotions erupted between us, moving from lost longing to desperate urges, and snap-shots flickered through my mind of everything he thought and felt. His cautious hopes and intense fears mixed with mine, bonding us together tighter than ever.

His lips grew hungrier on mine and he stopped to catch his breath. "Isobel," he whispered, closing his eyes, and then without warning, a bright flash of light shot between us, blasting us apart.

It was like lightning had struck, but instead of bolts of burning pain, our minds exploded with illumination that shot terror between us.

Ryan fell back against the door. "Did you see it?" he panted.

I swallowed hard. "Yes."

Fire. Screaming. Pain.

A vision of hell. A prophecy. And we were in the middle of it. Targets of a centuries old curse.

His shoulders sank. "We're fucked."

My eyes fell shut. "Yup."

"Ryan." Maureen's sharp voice passed through his door. "You'll be takin' the couch, laddy." Her direct tone confirmed her intention of keeping us moral.

"Got it," he called back to her. "We'll be out in a second."

He exhaled, looking into my eyes. "What do we do?"

I gazed at him as my throat tightened, knowing we were entering the battle of our lives. A war to keep us together and a fight that could tear us apart. Our next moves would be critical and each one was a possible landmine.

The images that had flashed between us played over and over in my mind. Fire. Screaming. Pain. I was sure one of the anguished faces I'd seen was Maeve's—death-like and tortured. She was caught in the abyss, withering away into nothing.

And we were next.

It was a prophecy. Clear as day.

"The curse is active," I stated. "It's only a matter of time before it takes us." I moved toward his door, rubbing my temples. "We need to figure out these Druids, their power. They're everywhere through Ireland's ancient history and there's only one person I know who has that type of knowledge."

"Yup. McGratt," Ryan said with a nod, following me out of his room.

We joined Maureen at the table and sat with heavy thumps. A wave of guilt washed over me as I noticed the stress deepening the lines in her face.

"I'm sorry about the trouble, Maureen." I avoided her eyes and gazed at her bookshelves.

"Nothin' I can't handle, dear. I'll protect you and Ryan with all me being." She reached across the table and squeezed my wrist. "Just tell me what I can do ta help."

I glanced at Ryan, wondering what he was willing to share with her, but then my eyes jumped back to her bookshelves. A thick, old book with weathered lettering on its spine caught my attention. The title blasted its name into my brain—*Ancient Order of Druids.*

I leapt to my feet and flew to the bookcase. "Can I look at this?" I turned back to Maureen as I reached for the aged book.

She pushed herself to standing as if startled and her eyes bored into mine. "'Tis the book of the Druids. Sure, I forgot it was even there." Her knuckles whitened on the back of her chair.

"May I?" I glanced to Ryan as I reached closer to it.

He sat up taller, watching me as if I'd be burned if I touched the book.

She nodded with unusual reluctance and I pulled the book out from its snug position. Its firm resistance proved it was quite comfortable staying where it was.

"Handle it with care." Maureen loosened her grip on her chair. "It's showing signs of age like some others of us."

Maureen fidgeted with her tea cup, moving it around the table as if looking for the right placement of it. Her skittish behavior made it seem as if she didn't want me to look in the book, which of course made me all the more curious.

I brought the book over to the couch and plopped down. Its weight in my lap measured its wisdom by the kilo. I was afraid to open it for fear of unleashing something I wouldn't be able to control or understand. Instead, I gently stroked the cover.

"Can we borrow this, Maureen?" I asked. "I'll take good care of it. I promise."

The information in the book could be crucial to understanding of our next moves. And combined with Paul's knowledge, we might actually have something to work with.

Maureen's eyes darted to Ryan's in silent question and he nodded back to her.

"Of course," she said. "Sure ya can." She walked to the coat closet and fumbled within. "Here, let me wrap it in this." She wound a woolen scarf around it and then placed it in a cracked leather satchel that must have been fifty years old. "There. Should be safe enough." She squeezed the bag to her chest. "It holds centuries of truths. Be cautious with it. Please."

"I promise." I took the bag as she handed it to me, her eyes on Ryan the whole time.

I couldn't be positive, but I thought I might have caught a nod between them—one that didn't include me.

Plowing through the ancient book of Druids became an immediate need, an insatiable urge. It made spending the night at Maureen's before going to see Paul tolerable. Plus, her bangers and mash were unparalleled anywhere in Ireland and the soul food was just what I needed.

Ryan cozied on the couch with me, just close enough without actually touching and I couldn't help but think we had our own personal curse. The one where we could be together but forever apart. Maybe the Druid curse was responsible for this too, creating a rift in time that opened when we touched. I prayed that ending it would also make us safe in holding each other.

I took the book out of its secure housing. I cracked the cover open, and the sound of the binding and smell of the musty pages set an eerie tone like we were entering a sacred place rarely visited.

As I turned each delicate page, our eyes widened at the detailed illustrations. At first, the ancient sketches depicted dark-robed men worshipping nature through fire and star-gazing, oak forests and streams. Gentle rhythms of the earth wove throughout the rituals of the Druids. Certain aspects of nature highlighted their worship, most profoundly the summer solstice. Its repeated mention and ample celebrations proved its position as a pinnacle in their devotion.

But the deeper we moved through the pages, the more intense the images became. The robed men held stern gazes and broad postures of control. Some pictures suggested rituals of human sacrifice in attempts to predict the future.

They appeared unhappy, judging the way things were evolving around them, moving from honoring the delicate balance of nature to a detached, modern system of controlling nature and manipulating it. The new way of life around them, modernization of tools, farming, and trade, killed the symbiosis of the elements and the heartbeat of the earth faded under their feet.

I turned to Ryan. "There's something here. Do you feel it? It's like, their full story is just beneath the surface." I closed the book and placed my hands on its cover. A profound sense that the Druids were all around us filled my mind. "Do you think they really performed human sacrifices? I've never heard that before."

Ryan reached for the book, as if to touch it, but then pulled his hand back. "I don't know. They were mostly known as peaceful scholars, but I guess history has to add some drama along the way." He inched back into the pillows on the couch. "Though, I have to admit, there was one childhood story of the Druids that scared the livin' shit outta me. Kids used to play it up on Hallows Eve." He bared his teeth with a cringe.

"What was it?" I pressed.

"The wicker man."

I pushed the book off my lap onto the couch next to me and swallowed. "The wicker man? That sounds creepy."

"Ya, it was. I've tried to forget it. Childhood has a way of making goblins and things that go bump in the night larger than life." He cracked his knuckles.

"Tell me the story." I sat up taller.

"We'll probably find somethin' about it in the book." He cleared his throat. "But story goes the Druids would use human sacrifice as a way of seeing future events more clearly, like the book says."

"So they *did* do human sacrifice," I interrupted.

"Who knows. The story's an old legend," he continued. "They were prophets and seers, and used these rituals as a way to gain sight into coming events. They'd build a huge wicker man, made of wood, hollow. His face was contorted and monstrous with giant twigs lifting off the top of his head like crazed hair. I swear it chased me in my nightmares my entire youth." He huffed. "His fingers were long branches that reached for miles, able to catch anything in his path."

"What was he made for?" I asked with a shudder.

"They would fill the wicker man with their sacrifices. Dozens of people, criminals and innocents. Then they would light it on fire."

"Holy shit." I dropped my head into my hand. Medieval torture techniques never ended with their creativity in brutal deaths. "I seriously hope that's not true."

"Ya. Goes back to whoever it was that wrote the history. The church was known for skewing the truth for their own gain. Whatever their agenda was." His shoulders lifted. "Probably trying to discredit the Druids as a religious order." He looked at the book. "The Druids didn't leave any written accounts of themselves, so no one will ever really know."

Closing my eyes, I allowed the history of the Druids into my soul in hopes of allowing their truth to flow through me. I pictured them in their robes, worshipping the earth around them, but other images interfered with my thoughts, pushing away the ancient Druids. The new images flashed stronger in my mind, leaving no doubt of their message.

My eyes burst open.

The clearing. The boulders at the clearing. They flashed in my mind, jolting me up straight.

I pulled my legs in under me and turned to Ryan. "It's at the clearing. The answers to all of this. There was something deep in that passageway and it's been haunting me ever since." I glanced at the book again. "I've been drawn back there for years. And now I think there's been a purpose behind it. Something more that I need to discover."

Ryan glanced back toward Maureen's bedroom door, to be sure she was still asleep and undisturbed. "The Druids aren't to be messed with, Isobel." His eyes fell to the book again, as if it might be dangerous. "They're one of the earliest orders on record, from thousands of years ago. It was believed they held mystical power. They were seers too."

My air sucked in.

They were seers. Like us.

"I knew it. It's all connected somehow!" I wiggled in my seat with unleashed enthusiasm.

"No. It's not exciting," he barked. "It's dangerous."

His tone hit me like a slap in the face. Here we go again, I thought. Ryan's reluctance to face all of this. To better understand our gifts. To bring balance back—to everything. I couldn't handle the roadblock, and plowed through it.

"Ryan. I know this could be dangerous..."

"Will be dangerous," he interjected.

"Fine. Will be dangerous. But back at Rockfleet, Maeve was dying and the curse hasn't ended." I glared at the book as if it taunted me. "And I believe it falls on me to end it. Now."

I'd been given enough clues to know I held responsibility in this event. It was as if I'd been prepped for it my whole life. My visions had been a curse for as long as I could remember, but now, they were my gift. They were a portal for me to connect events through time that the Druids had broken.

I needed to make the next move. To take the information I'd been given and act on it.

And I intended to waste no time.

Ryan was right though. The danger was real. I could be lost in the abyss of time or worse. I could end up dead. I had no clue who might try to stop me or what I might face, but that wasn't' enough to derail me.

I was ready to take the risk.

The biggest risk of my life.

CHAPTER 9

My restless sleep filled Ryan's room with flying ancient books swooping past me, flapping their pages in my face, and cloaked shadows lurking in every dark corner. But the worst of it was the lumbering wicker man—stretched tall and reaching high into the sky, moving through my safe places, scooping up my loved ones into his hollows for future sacrifice. Gram struggled from being crushed in the lower part of his leg, while Declan and Michelle clung to each other in his chest cavity. Down his right arm, I caught a glimpse of Jayne's sneering face.

Blinking into the morning rays through the curtains, my pasty eyes proved my lack of restful sleep and I rubbed the fog from them.

Our plan was for an early start at the university to find Paul. I dragged myself out of Ryan's cozy bed. Cracking his door open, I peered out and caught a glimpse of him sleeping on the couch.

His resting vulnerability sent butterflies through my stomach and my eyes moved along the lean muscles in his arm, hanging off the side, and then along his stubbled jawline. His features enticed me in every way and their power was enough to erase my annoyance at his reluctance to pursue our mission. However maddening his discouragement was, I still couldn't help but want him with every ounce of my being.

Maureen's door cracked open. "Mornin' dear."

She had the kettle on in the same breath.

I watched her move through the morning rituals as Ryan resisted the early call of the day. Their routines fell into place in a symbiotic flow of daily tasks and family traditions as I watched their comfortable dance together. Coffee and tea, porridge and cream, gazes out the window at the awakening day.

"Let me know what ya learn from Professor McGratt, will ya dear?" Maureen asked. "I'm keen ta hear what he knows of the Druids."

Her comments motivated us to get going and Ryan went around back to pull the truck out. I crossed to the couch to find the book and glanced around the coffee table and surrounding floor area. I lifted the couch pillows and searched for it further. As I turned in confusion, I saw it at the hearth where the last bit of smoldering coal sent a swirling trail of smoke up the flue.

At the side of the hearth, the wool scarf and leather satchel waited on standby and I grabbed the long woolen wrapping. As I reached for the book, I noticed strange ash on the top and instinctively brushed at it only to find half-burned sprigs of herbs around it. One of Maureen's mortar and pestles sat off to the side, still holding some mixed leaves and powders.

I turned to Maureen with questions that scrambled in my mouth, vying for priority of being asked. The main question being, "What the hell is this? What's going on?" But just as our eyes met, she turned on her heel and went out the back door, leaving all of my questions unanswered.

And leaving me with several new ones.

With the book half-wrapped in the dark woolen scarf, I stuffed it into the worn brown satchel as I hurried outside to the waiting truck.

"You okay?" Ryan asked.

"Um, something kinda strange," I looked back toward the cottage, glancing around for Maureen. "The book was by the hearth and had some weird ashes on it. Did you put it there?" I watched him as he pulled the truck out of the yard and onto the narrow green road.

"No. Didn't touch it." He shook his head. "I'm sure it's fine."

"No, like, someone put it there. And did stuff to it. It looked like herbs or something had been placed around it." I moved the cracked-leather satchel to the floor at my feet.

"Probably just cinders from the hearth." He brushed it off like it wasn't of interest.

My thumping heart told me different though.

We drove along the Spiddal road heading into Galway City, and I gazed out on the bay any time it came into view. The day was clear enough to see across to County Clare and I imagined the view of the majestic Cliffs of Moher that overlooked the Atlantic, just out of sight along the horizon.

Traffic slowed our progress as we entered the city limits. The university wasn't much farther.

"I think Paul will be a little surprised to see me." I smirked. "He probably thinks I'll be stuck on that island until I'm twenty, at least."

I shook my head, thinking of Jayne still trapped there. Not a moment went by that I didn't cringe at the thought of her rotting in purgatory. I'd have to make contact soon, before she lost hope. Hope was all she had.

"Yeah, I think he's kinda used to surprises with us," Ryan joked. "Plus, it's time he gave me an update on the dig site by the house. There's been more activity lately but no information."

"I wonder if they've found any new artifacts. I mean, anything could be buried there." I leaned in my seat as Ryan turned the truck into NUIG and drove toward the lot near Paul's history building.

I thought back to when we excavated the O'Shaughnessy's crate—the one that held family treasures, but more so, the ring. The findings were incredible and somehow my visions brought us to it. I hoped they would work again to help with our current situation.

Ryan parked the truck and I turned and looked up the large

granite steps leading to the gothic building. I grabbed the satchel and hopped out. Campus was quiet with only a few summer students moving about, which helped me feel inconspicuous.

We moved through the echoing halls, passing dusty cases of archaeological finds and academic awards, and then slowed our pace as we approached Paul's office door.

"I hope he's in there," I mumbled as I rapped my knuckles across his name on the opaque window.

"Yup." Paul's voice travelled out to us and I looked at Ryan. He nudged his chin at me to go on.

As I pushed the door open, my heart rate shot through the roof. Seeing Paul again was more profound than I had prepared myself for. His deep connection to Maeve was unfathomable for starters, but also his witness of the mystical events surrounding her disappearance made him more complex. Just as my eyes met his, he flew out of his seat.

His chair fell behind him, banging off the wall, and he leaned forward with both hands on his desk, staring. His lip twitched and his eyes squinted. He moved back from his desk and hit his back against the wall like he'd seen a ghost.

"Um, Paul," I stuttered. "Is this a bad time?"

"Jesus Christ! Bloody hell!" His hands moved through his hair.

In a quick attempt at escape, I turned and smacked right into Ryan's chest. I pushed to get him to back up out of the door as Paul's voice assaulted me further.

"What the fuckin' hell?" His voice burst through me but this time the tone had lightened. "I thought you were fuckin' dead. Word is out that ya drowned. Jesus! It's like I'm seeing yer ghost."

He pushed off the wall and came around to me with open arms. He hugged me tight as he spoke to Ryan.

"Best goddamn surprise I've had in a while, lad. How'd ye pull it off?" He released me and stepped back for a better look. "Ya faked your death? Brilliant."

"Maureen got the ring to her on the island. It's a long story, but, yeah. She escaped," Ryan stated.

"That's brilliant, Isobel. Fair play ta ya," he chuffed.

I smiled, remembering every detail of the great escape, but then the elation moved back to concern as I remembered Maeve's condition in the vision that ensued.

"I thought we'd make it to you before the news of my disappearance," I said. "Sorry to give you such a shock."

He looked at the dated satchel hanging from my shoulder and the acclaimed historian in him emerged. It was clear he knew something of interest could be concealed within.

"No worries," he said. "I spend enough of my time studying the long-gone. It's nice to have a solid reminder of what is here and now. It's good to see you. Both of you."

Paul paused and studied our faces. The wheels turned in his mind and I couldn't be sure what he was thinking, but the tense muscles in his face showed a deep level of calculation.

He pointed to my satchel.

"So, what's in the bag?"

Paul paced from his desk to the window so many times I lost count. It was either the vivid images I'd described of Maeve's suffering or the details of the curse from the Druids that wound him up. Each tale turned his face ashen, and combined, turned him into a nervous wreck.

"Jesus." He paced more, searching for words. "But the ring brought some life back into her?" He leaned on his desk, waiting for reassurance.

"Yes. Definitely," I stated. "It was a game changer. But it wasn't enough. Our gifts are weakening. And there are disruptions that seem to be tied to it." I glanced at his cell phone. "Have you noticed problems with your technology?"

Paul grabbed his phone and dropped it again like it was worthless. "Feckin' things useless. All apps are frozen and can't pick up a signal for miles."

"Well, there's more, too. I keep having flashes from the clearing. Like it holds a secret it's ready to reveal." I dropped the strap of the satchel off my shoulder.

Paul cleared folders and trinkets to the side of his desk, making room for the bag. His eyes locked on mine as he held his breath.

I placed the satchel on the desk and slowly pulled the book out. I unraveled the protective scarf from around it and placed the heavy book on top for cushioning.

Paul's jaw fell open as he stared at it. His eyes lifted to mine, and then Ryan's. I caught an unexpected look in his eye, one of question, as if he was measuring us for how much we knew about the book.

"Where did you get this?" he asked.

Ryan stepped closer. "It's Maureen's. She's had it for as long as I can remember."

Paul's hand went to his mouth and pulled down to the end of his chin. "Well, you keep the surprises comin', you two. And this one's even bigger than returning from the dead."

"How so?" I asked.

Paul leaned over the book, inspecting it as he opened the top drawer of his desk and pulled out latex gloves. Snapping the purple gloves at his wrists, he reached for the cover. "Can I touch it?"

I nodded.

He checked the condition of the masterfully-crafted cover and binding and I watched his focus as he absorbed every detail. His awe was spellbinding, and raised my guard more with each passing second.

"It's a treasure," he spoke out. "The Druids were literate but were prevented by doctrine from recording their history and knowledge. Only a few original written accounts exist in the world, thought to be lost." He paused. "And we are looking at one of them."

A shudder ran through him.

I stared as he cracked the book open for a peek inside.

"They were a highly sophisticated religious system dating back thousands of years, to before Christianity. Some carried the songs and legends of the tribe, while others were philosophers and teachers. But the most revered of the order were the seers, the Ovates." His eyes tracked each page as he turned them with delicate precision.

I bent in and looked at the pages to see what he was seeing. "How do we know which sect is behind the curse?" I asked. "They're the ones who want to stop the progression of time, to preserve Gaelic Ireland."

Paul paused and lifted his eyes to mine.

I continued. "They knew of Maeve's prophecies and her knowledge of future events. They would have seen her as an Ovate, no?"

Paul held my gaze while thinking, then nodded.

"Right. And once they understood her power, they wanted it for themselves. That way, they would have full control of time." He paused and narrowed his eyes. "They would need to stop all Ovates in order to achieve their goal."

My breath stopped. "So, we're all in danger. With Maeve being their immediate, prime target."

Paul nodded in silence.

I continued, "If they stopped her, they would stop the time portal she moved through, closing off the possibilities of seeing the future. And in their minds, closing off the future all together. Stopping time in its tracks."

My words sounded jumbled once they left my mouth. I didn't know how to accurately describe my theory because it was just too vast with so many unknowns.

"I think the clearing might be the portal," I added. "Hidden in the boulders, there was like, a passage. If we go there…"

Paul slammed the book shut, making me jump. His jaw tensed as he considered his next words.

"And what do you intend to do there? Disrupt history? Set a ripple in time that will impact every aspect of existence?" His tone bit at me. "You're not unlike Maeve in your grand notions."

He had loved Maeve. It was likely he still did, and more so, probably resented her for leaving him and staying in the past. He'd been tormented since the moment of her disappearance. I thought back to the hoard of flowers, years worth, hidden in the boulders at the clearing. He hadn't let her go.

Paul was connected to this tale as much as any of us. We were intertwined in ways we didn't fully understand yet and together, we had a chance at setting things right.

"Will you help us?" I asked.

He glanced at the book and then back at us. "I suppose I don't really have a choice." He hesitated and considered his words while his eyes narrowed, measuring us. "And based on everything you've just told me, I have a hunch about something that could be huge."

I pressed my hand on the book and leaned across his desk. “Like what?”

He glanced at us and then out the window. “Who’s ready for another field study?”

CHAPTER 10

Paul's cryptic messages about his ideas on the clearing left us starving for more information, but he kept the details just out of our reach. His discretion made me think I might need to be more guarded with my own plans and intimate knowledge as well. It was clear to me he had an ulterior motive.

Paul still wanted Maeve.

Any time her name was mentioned it was as if his fight or flight mechanism tripped into gear and all his senses piqued to high alert. Maybe he was scheming a way to get her back to the present. That would explain his hidden agenda. And maybe it wasn't such a bad idea. She was dying back at Rockfleet anyway.

I bit at my cuticles, trying to determine if I was being selfish or doing the right thing. This was the teetering point I always felt myself on.

"Well, this is the first time I've actually felt nervous about going to the clearing." I turned to Ryan and he glanced at me, then back at the road.

"Welcome to the club. I nearly lose my shit every time," he huffed.

I chuckled, appreciating his honesty.

"Everything's kind of overlapping and entwining like a rat's nest," I mumbled. "I'm losing focus on what's actually happening. Ya know?" I dug into my backpack for a water and took quick inventory of the other contents—flashlight, first aid kit, extra batteries, power bars. "What are you hoping will happen?"

He reached for my water and took a gulp.

"I guess I want to feel normal again. Well, for once," he said. "I want to be able to relax and let my guard down. These visions have taken over our lives. We just need some control, some balance, I guess." He looked at me for a reaction and I nodded. "I want us to be able to be together. Like, without worry."

I reached for him but stopped just before touching.

He was right. I wanted to be able to be with him too. Without worry of blasting to another time or seeing frightening images.

Feeling his thoughts when we kissed though, that was wondrous. I smiled guiltily as my eyes travelled across his body.

He grinned, feeling my eyes all over him.

"What are *you* hoping will happen?" he asked.

"Isn't that obvious?" I teased.

He tossed the water bottle at me.

"Fine," I conceded. "I want what you said too." I paused in thought. "And though I want to control our visions, I also want to be sure to keep them alive. Forever." I exhaled. "Since meeting you and Maureen, I've learned to actually love our gifts. They make us who we are. I'd never want to lose that."

A familiar boulder whizzed by with a painted greeting, 'Welcome to Ballycroy', awakening jitters in my stomach as we got closer to our destination.

"But I also feel a larger responsibility to all the seers, like Maeve, and Maureen, and even the Druids," I added. "To help bring balance back to it all. It's like everything became disconnected at some point—imbalance in nature, isolated human existence instead of clans, halted advancement of technology—and the pieces are crumbling all around us."

I pushed the water bottle back into my pack, pondering my words.

"That's what I want to accomplish," I continued. "I want to restore our gifts. I want the balance of nature to realign, including time moving forward as it was meant to. I want to rescue Maeve from the curse. And damn it, I want our modern conveniences to remain intact!" I let out a laugh.

Ryan huffed and pointed ahead as the jagged ramparts of Doona Castle came into view.

"All makes sense," he said. "I just have no idea how you can do all that."

"Yeah. Same." I glanced up the green hills in the direction of the clearing and imagined what might be in store for us.

"There's Paul's car. He's already here." Ryan parked next to it at the side of the church ruin by the ancient cemetery.

"Why is that not a shock." I felt a twinge of resentment that he got to the clearing before us and had to remind myself it wasn't a competition.

Or was it?

~

After surveying the coastline and surrounding area of Doona Castle with no sign of Paul, we started the trek up the green hills toward the clearing. The leather bag on my shoulder added fatigue to each vertical step from the weight of the contents inside—the book and its heavy substance.

The boulders of the clearing soon came into view and my steps lightened. Crouching by one of the largest boulders, Paul pulled notebooks and other items from his research bag. It was the same bag he used at the excavation site by Ryan's cottage, full of every tool of his trade.

I moved up behind him and spoke before I got too close, to avoid startling him.

"Got an early start?" I said.

He spun around like he'd been caught in the midst of a crime and I jumped back in alarm.

It wasn't Paul.

I staggered back from the shock and searched the rest of the clearing.

"Murt?" Ryan called out from behind me.

"How ya, Ryan. Isobel," Murt greeted us. "Sorry to surprise ya. Paul brought me along for field support."

I shook off my bewilderment and caught a glimpse of Paul coming out from behind another boulder, his expression locked in full focus on preparation of the site.

I wondered how much Paul had shared with Murt, and pushed down the feeling of betrayal that stung at me. Murt had proven himself a great archaeologist and historian at the dig back at Ryan's. But still. I couldn't help being protective of our mission.

"Oh, I just didn't expect to see anyone else here. Took me by surprise," I replied to Murt, pulling myself back together.

"I see ya made it," Paul called over to us. "Now, we'll need ta set our game plan, but first things first, ye must show me the passageway you spoke of."

I recoiled in response to his direction and straight away didn't like the shift in power. Paul had been invited along and now it seemed he was leading the expedition. I'd need to correct that immediately.

"I hadn't expected an addition to the team, Paul," I started. "No offense, Murt," I added with a nod to him. "I think we need to be clear on where this information starts and stops, and already it's moved beyond a scope I'm comfortable with." I held Paul's eyes.

He broke away from my glare after a moment and looked to Murt.

"My apologies, Isobel. I should have mentioned it to you," Paul said. "It's a knee-jerk reaction for me to reach out to Murt. He's a renowned expert in the field and I'd be lost without him."

Murt interjected, "Confidentiality is part of me work, Isobel. Whatever we find here will remain quiet until next steps are determined."

"And who determines those next steps?" I pressed.

"Well, you, of course," Paul added.

But, again, a nag in my gut sent my radar flashing. Something wasn't right.

I stood without flinching, uncertain of my next move.

"It's okay. I get it." Murt started repacking his bag. "These things can be delicate, I know. And you didn't expect me. I understand." He looked to Paul and nodded. "No worries. You call me when you need me."

Aw, shit. Now it felt like we were losing an important part of the team. It had just taken me off guard, was all.

"No, stay. Sorry. I just wasn't prepared to grow the team. But I can see the value in it now." I pulled some of his instruments out of the bag again. It was clear they would be useful. "Sorry for any offense."

"None taken." Murt smiled.

It would have pained him deeply to have had to leave, I knew that. But he was willing to do it and I appreciated it.

I went over to Ryan and asked, "You okay with this?"

"Yeah, I guess. But I definitely had the same initial reaction as you," he said. "I'm sure Paul will be more cautious in the future."

I turned to Paul and caught the worry lines moving across his forehead. The anxiety in his eyes proved he didn't want us to lose faith in him. He knew we were his link to Maeve and all the mysticism around her and this clearing. The last thing he would want would be to feel left out or left behind.

I moved closer to Paul and nodded for him to follow. Ryan and Murt stayed close behind.

"You've actually been extremely close to it many times. It's almost as if you were drawn to it somehow," I said to Paul as we stepped closer to the two boulders that sheltered the crevice.

"What do you mean?" Paul asked.

I reached into the space between the boulders and pulled out a handful of dried bouquets and ribbons—all left over the years by Paul.

His eyes met mine with wide wonder.

"In there?" he asked with a stunned ring to his voice.

Just as I nodded yes, a waft of stale air pushed out from deep within the crevice. We all fell back from the pungent stench of death. I struggled to suppress my gag reflex as my eyes burned from the foul assault on our senses.

"What the hell is that?" I choked.

"It's hell itself, lassie." Murt winced. "Belched right in our faces, it did."

His eerie words sent a chill up my spine. It wasn't something I would have expected a man of his background to say.

"Maybe an animal's using it for his burrow?" I suggested.

Paul pulled a tissue from his pocket and covered his nose and mouth with it. Leaning in for a better look, he turned back to us and said, "It's not the stink of an animal's den or rotting carcass." He peered in further, then looked back at me with unblinking eyes. "It's much older than that."

I stepped back as a sick reminder of the omen twisted in my gut.

"It's a warning," I whispered.

~

We were treading on dangerous ground. The warning of death was enough to send any mortal running for the hills. For their life.

But not me.

This was the gateway to everything. Its mystery called to me from behind the stench of rotting hell. Others might stay away after encountering such an assault, but me, I took it as a challenge.

"Give me the flashlight." I reached back to Ryan.

He pulled the bright yellow palm-sized light from the pack, but before he reached me with it, Murt had the handle of a huge, box-like flashlight in my hand and clicked it on. The beam that shone from it was wide and bright beyond belief.

I nodded, glad to have Murt here. It was true his equipment brought the expedition to the next level. I just hoped his experience would do the same.

I aimed the massive beam of light down into the deep crevice. The narrow passageway turned, leaving me unsure of how far it actually went.

"I just need to squeeze down there for a better look. Tough to say how deep it goes." I wiggled in between the boulders, crushing several of the bouquet stems that had accumulated over the years. I glanced back at Paul in apology.

"Wait. You might slip or get stuck." Ryan reached for me. "There's no way to know how deep that goes."

"Ryan..." I resisted.

"No, he's right, Isobel," Paul interjected. "We need to use caution. Ropes for starters."

Murt was already at the gear bag, digging out a colorful paracord typically used for rock climbing. Paul motioned to him with a cupped hand at his forehead and Murt nodded, pulling out a couple head-lamps as well.

"Fine day for spelunking, I'd say," he joked as he tied the rope around my waist.

I looked back into the darkness of the hole and watched glistening water trickling down the stones on each side. A shudder ran through me, trying to discourage me from going down there, but I shook it off and shimmied closer to the opening.

"Don't go too far. Just far enough to tell us what you can see around the bend," Paul instructed.

I scooched along the damp rocks and moved into the dark opening. Shifting from stone to stone, I went deeper in, keeping a strong hold on each rock that jutted out or stuck up from beneath me. Water had eroded them to slippery smooth, so there wasn't much purchase. I continued my subtle movement into the gateway to hell.

"Can you see anything?" a voice called down to me, making me jump out of my skin.

I fumbled with the flashlight hanging from a utility belt Paul had clipped around me.

"Hang on," I whispered back.

I aimed the beam of light ahead and it bounced back off the sleek wet stones, blinding me. I lowered the light again and blinked through the spots and streaks burned onto my retinas.

Keeping the light lower this time, I raised it enough to see ahead, and angled it to the left in the direction of a natural curve in the subterranean stones. My breath caught in my throat at what I saw.

I kicked against the wet rocks beneath me to push back up to safety but instead slipped further in.

"Pull me up!" I yelled.

The slack rope tightened, stabilizing me.

"We got you," they called back.

I pushed and pressed my way back up through the dank passageway while keeping my eyes fixed down the crevice, certain creatures of hell would grab me at any moment.

"Faster!" I called. My voice shook and echoed through the vast abyss below me.

They pulled and I kicked my way to the opening where daylight reached for me.

"Quick! Get me out," I begged.

"We got you." Paul reached under my arms and pulled me all the way out.

I twisted around and wrapped him in a desperate embrace of relief. Ryan paced just out of my reach with a grimace of jealousy that pained me.

"You're shaking like a leaf. What did you see?" Paul pressed for details.

After several deep inhales, I finally caught my breath enough to speak. I looked back toward the opening to be sure nothing was reaching out for me—it was a true cavern of nightmares.

"It opens up after the first bend," I panted. "Like the entryway to something even bigger."

"And..." Murt bounced in place.

"There are guardians," I whispered.

CHAPTER 11

Nervous energy charged the air in the clearing as explorer gear flew out of bags all around us. We reached for the pieces that made sense for our own needs.

I grabbed a headlamp, extra rope, a small bag, and water. Ryan had the same but added some tools to his belt, like a small pick axe and a hand trowel. Paul and Murt filled backpacks with electronic devices for measuring who-knows-what and small brushes, magnifiers, and fine pointed tools. Ropes hung from everyone's waists and extra batteries were loaded into every pocket.

"Guardian statues are typical protectors of ancient tombs," Paul informed us. "But they could also be a sign of a secret place of worship. We won't know until we pass them."

I hoisted my belt in nervous anticipation of seeing the disturbing statues again. Their huge eyes bored right into my soul, unblinking, and their cloaks added a haunting element of secrecy and sorcery. Whatever it was they were guarding shot fear through me like poison.

Paul moved to the opening, preparing to enter.

"Me first." The words popped out of my mouth before I approved them.

But it was true.

I should be the first to enter. No question about it. But I had no idea what to expect and my bones jittered at the thought of what I might encounter.

"Then Ryan," I added.

I didn't mean to disrespect Paul in any way, but he was lucky to be here at all. This discovery had everything to do with Ryan and me. With Maeve. All of the seers of Ireland.

Paul was here for Maeve as well, I had to remember that. But his intentions were different from ours. And I wasn't completely clear on them.

"Sound. You're right." Paul stepped back to make room for us. "I'm just a bit eager is all."

I moved into the crevice and aimed my huge light beam down the passageway. Though I knew what to expect around the deep bend, my bones still shook within me, causing my entire body to shiver and twitch. I turned back to Ryan for encouragement.

"Let's do this." He shimmied up close behind me. "I won't let you out of my sight."

"Same." I smiled.

His eyes moved over my body. “Your ass is smokin’ in that adventure gear, by the way,” he whispered. “Must be why I’m followin’ you around like a lost puppy.”

I threw a small stone at his leg but in truth, the distraction of his comment was exactly what I needed before lowering myself into the dank, dripping black hole.

"Wait for us at the guardians," Paul called to me. "We need to move slowly with caution at every stage."

He was right. There was no telling what hid beyond the guardians. Booby traps maybe. Endless pits of despair. Zombies. I squeezed my eyes shut and opened them again. Clearly I'd seen too many action movies.

But in reality, safety was the primary concern. Rocks could shift from centuries of erosion and crush us, or worse. It was possible we could be the first to have stepped foot in here in the past five hundred years. Anything could happen.

I moved my feet into the opening and inched my way in. Positioning each foot securely, I lowered myself along the narrow passage toward the bend to the left. As I reached the turn, I looked back for Ryan who was close behind me.

"Feckin' slippery," he panted from the exertion necessary to prevent sliding all the way to the pits of hell.

"I know. Makes it near impossible," I agreed.

A pebble bounced past us, proving that Paul and Murt were on the move.

Eager for Ryan to see the guardians before the others joined us, I waved him to follow me around the bend. His breath tickled my neck as we squeezed through the narrow curve in the passageway.

This time, I felt the bravery of a tour guide giddy to show hidden treasure. I lifted my flashlight and sent the light beam ahead, illuminating the massive stone figures.

"Shit!" Ryan stopped short. "Ya coulda warned me. Jazus. They're huge. And haunting." His hand ran through his hair as he looked back for Paul and Murt.

"There's no way to describe them accurately. You just need to see them," I said.

He stepped closer again and shone his own light at the faces of the guardians. Our two powerful beams lit up the space behind the statues, exposing a larger tunnel.

"Bah." Ryan shot his voice into the darkness to measure distance. The blunt sound echoed into the tunnel and travelled into oblivion.

Movement behind us made me turn my head as Paul and Murt caught up to us. I angled my light back at the statues for them to see and my eye caught sudden motion from behind them. I tracked my beam to follow the rustle and it trailed down through the tunnel in an instant.

"What the hell was that?" I turned to Ryan to be sure he saw it too.

"Hmm? What?" He bent in to follow my beam.

"I don't know. Nothing, maybe," I murmured.

My spine tingled as I second-guessed our mission. Was it even right for us to be here? Were our intentions just? What if we were about to disturb history and change the course of events?

I hoisted my tool belt and the accessories swung at my hips. As unsure as I was about entering such a sacred space, I couldn't stop the drive to move forward.

"Keepers of the Ovate Guard," Paul commented. His flashlight shone into the eyes of the closest one. "Pristine condition. Thousands of years old judging from the style of carving and the ancient facial features." His voice caught in his throat and he cleared it with a cough. "A discovery of a lifetime, one I couldn't have imagined in my wildest dreams."

Murt lit up the second statue. "The Keepers protect the sanctuary of rebirth."

"What?" I turned my light on Murt, half-blinding him. "Sorry." I clicked it off and hung it from a carabiner on my belt. Pulling the strap of my headlamp over my hair, I turned the smaller, less cumbersome, light on.

"Just keep your chin up when talking to someone. That way the light won't shine into their eyes," Murt instructed.

Paul stepped closer to one of the ghoulish guardians. "The sanctuary of rebirth. The Druid ritual sent men into the dark chamber, devoid of all senses, and when they came out, they were never the same again." He nudged his light forward toward the tunnel. "Shall we?"

My flight response set my heart pounding. I couldn't imagine walking into that dark tunnel with no idea of what could be lurking in its alcoves. Maybe it would just lead to a large open area, like a meeting space for a secret society. The guardians were just there to scare off any intruders.

I glanced at Ryan to see how he was feeling about entering the cavernous passage. The sweat beading on his brow left no uncertainty.

"Hold onto the wall so you don't slip," I whispered. "It looks like we can fit through without a problem."

I moved my head around to get my light to shine on every surface. Bats and spiders were unwelcome as far as I was concerned.

"Feel each step before you take it. Just in case there's any drop off." Paul's voice straightened my spine.

"Got it," I called back through clenched teeth.

Ryan and I moved through the darkness that reached deeper and deeper into the earth. The further we went, the less moisture seeped off the walls, making it easier to navigate. The sound of each step reverberated through the silent space, which was otherwise grave-like. After several minutes of slow progress, the side walls opened up, exposing what seemed to be a massive room.

"It's like a chamber or something," I whispered back. "I need more light."

Ryan lifted his headlamp in the direction of the chamber as I reached for the huge flashlight hanging from my belt. Paul and Murt joined us with their lights and between the four of us we illuminated the space around us.

"Nobody move!" Paul commanded.

I jumped out of my skin and searched all around me for either a venomous creature or the living dead. My bones rattled within me, causing my teeth to chatter.

"We mustn't disturb a thing," he continued while staring in awe. "It's a pristine archaeological find that must be…"

"Like hell." I walked into the space, ready to explore every inch of it. "Look at all the small doors in the walls." My eyes moved across the back of the chamber, noticing some openings between some of the doors.

I stepped around a center table-like structure, an altar maybe, and looked into the openings more closely with my light.

"Shit!" I jumped back as I held eye contact with the hollow orbs of a skull. An entire pile of skulls actually.

"It's a catacomb," Ryan said. "An ancient burial chamber."

"Right," Paul agreed. "Only, more." He stepped toward the altar and inspected it. His hand moved across the top and down along the side. "There's ancient writing carved here." His finger traced the lettering.

A wave of nausea threatened my composure as I stepped away from the cavity of skulls. With hands to knees, I dropped my head low.

"You okay?" Ryan stepped closer, then his head dropped too.

A slow moan moved through the chamber, carrying with it the stench of death. I dry heaved and hurried toward the tunnel to get away from the eerie groan.

"It's air, moving through the stones and the passageways," Paul said, lifting his arm to cover his nose and mouth.

But the moan grew louder as the foul stench whirled around us in hazy bursts of mist. The beams from our flashlights thickened the mist, making it impossible to see each other.

I called out to Ryan and reached for him. Stepping forward, I searched blindly for any contact with him. Just as I was about to cry out his name, a sense of calm coursed through my veins, dropping my heart rate to a low, steady rhythm.

And then, with a final blink, my vision took me.

The beam of light from my headlamp twisted and curled into a cone shape. My eyes strained to follow it into a vortex of swirling mist and harrowing sounds of ancient flutes and rhythmic drums.

Gazing into chaos, I found a zone of clarity that the mist avoided and moved around. Focusing down the funnel, I reeled back in horror at images of trapped men burning, screaming and writhing in agony.

Squeezing my eyes shut, I willed away the vision and opened them again only to see an unknown person emerging from the catacombs, blinking into the light of a new day. I squinted for a better look at the face and jolted as I recognized Maureen in their aging eyes. Blinking to clear my vision, I watched again as the face shifted and Maeve appeared to me. It was like the mysterious person represented all of the Ovates.

My vision shot images of the seers at me and all I felt was fear and an urge to run. Then the apparition of Maeve moved toward me. She held my eyes with hers and the corners of her mouth turned up in a grin of recognition. She reached her hands out in front of her and placed her palms together. A steady beam of light shone from her fingertips and she moved her hands until the light shined on a unique Celtic symbol carved in stone. She nodded at me and then faded.

I scrambled toward her and ran through her mist, smacking right into Ryan. He caught me before I fell back and his thoughts exploded in my mind. Every bit of his focus was on a beam of light. His eyes had tracked it but it became lost in the mist.

"You saw it too?" I shrieked. "The light?"

He released me and stepped back. "Yes. What was it?"

"You saw something?" Murt interrupted us.

I shot a stifling glance to Ryan, cautious of how much to share with Murt, and said, "Yeah, so much mist. That was just weird. I still feel sick from it." I reached for my stomach for emphasis.

"Let's get out of here." Paul waved for us to follow him. "We have plenty to discuss and we can come back with better gear."

"But the vaults," Murt blurted out. "We need to open one. We need to—"

"No, Murt. Now is not the time. This space is sacred and must be respected as such," Paul stated.

Murt angled his light back toward the small doors in the far wall and anger grimaced his face.

Paul's response to Murt settled my nervous jitters, proving he understood the delicate nature of what we were doing. It was as if Murt's impatience focused only on an end prize. Treasure. And I was sure he hoped to become famous by it.

It made him appear like an amateur though. And the expedition didn't need that kind of focus, at all. If anything, we'd likely leave everything undisturbed, if I had my way.

I followed Paul and made sure Ryan was right behind me. I was happy to leave Murt at the back as sweep. Let the curse or the stank of hell catch *him*, not us.

Though my wicked thoughts made me smile, I continued to look back to keep an eye on him and I was right to. He fell back more than once, aiming his light in every direction like he was searching for something.

"You comin', Murt? Wouldn't want to be left behind, I'm sure," I called back to him.

He shot a glare of annoyance my way, one that stung, and followed more closely after that.

We shimmied up the wet walls of the narrow passage, leaving the Keepers of the Ovate Guard to return to their loyal, steadfast duty.

One by one, we pressed out of the crevice and crawled into the clearing. After an extra moment of suspicious lagging, Murt was the last to emerge.

Sitting in the damp grass as mist coated our faces, we fumbled with our gear, creating a pile in the middle of us. Paul's hands shook as he unlatched the fasteners on his cargo vest. It was as if he needed extra room to breathe properly.

"Are you okay, Paul?" I asked as he reached into the breast pocket of his vest and pulled out a roll of hard candies.

"Glucose tabs." He nodded. "I'm low-blood-sugaring. Happens to me after...extreme situations." He popped two candies into his mouth.

"Yeah. Extreme's an understatement," Ryan added. "That's a goddamn discovery that'll wind up on the friggin' tellie. On every news report around the world."

"Exactly why we need to keep it quiet for now," I added. "Last thing we need is reporters and excavators and museums destroying every inch of it." I shuddered at the thought. "Right now, this is ours and I want to keep it that way for as long as possible."

"Agreed," Paul said while Ryan and Murt nodded their heads.

We sat in contemplative silence, each reliving our own highlights of the exploration. I stared at the crevice between the two boulders, still shocked at the vast secret they held within. Looking back toward Paul, I noticed his lips moving as his finger traced the air, like he was transcribing something.

The carvings on the altar.

Murt stood and began packing the gear into his huge travel bag. I scooted closer to Paul.

"Could you make out any of what it said, on the altar?" I looked at his hands as if I'd be able to read them. "What do you think it was?"

He popped another glucose tab and chewed on it. "It focused on the summer solstice. Repeating several times."

"Does that make any sense?" I pushed.

"It does, actually. The Druids worshipped the solstice. It was a most sacred time for them," he told me. "The longest day of the year carried great significance in their rituals. Particularly rebirth." He looked back toward the crevice. "There's more to this place than just a tomb. It was likely a sacred place of the Ovates. Where they came to practice their magic, to see the future. And to be reborn."

A violent shudder ran through me. "Can I have one of those?" I reached toward his pocket for a hit of glucose.

"We need to explore it more," he said as he reached for a candy for me. "See if there are any more words or symbols carved throughout. Maybe instructions or a map on how they performed their rituals."

"We could follow their directions and recreate their rituals." I stared at him as he passed me a candy. "It's like they wanted us to."

"Well, I hadn't gotten quite to that point. I was thinking more like learning more about their customs. But now that you mention it..." He paused to let me fill in the blanks. "It wouldn't seem that far-fetched considering the stuff you're capable of conjuring."

My eyes widened.

The clearing was a portal. I'd known it.

But I had no idea that it was only the tip of the iceberg. And now, we were all traipsing on mystical ground that echoed through eternity, connecting us all.

"Help me!"

My head spun toward the muffled sound—an eerie cry.

A woman's voice.

But there was no one there and no one else seemed to hear it. I stared in the direction of the spine-chilling sound.

Directly into the darkness of the crevice.

CHAPTER 12

Eight days until the summer solstice and counting.

Ryan cracked the door to his room to wake me and I rolled over in resistance.

"Rise and shine." He crept into the room and crawled onto the bed. In slow motion, he moved over me and hovered in a plank position just above me. The urge to grab hold of him awoke all of my senses to high alert.

"Hi." I smiled into his face while restraining my legs from wrapping around him.

"Coffee?"

"Yeah," I nodded. "Waking up this early isn't natural. I just want to stay here with you," I whined.

He moved his face over mine, so close but not quite touching, and lowered his body to mine, just out of reach. "What I could do to you," he whispered.

"Do," I begged, lifting my chin to reach him.

His biceps quivered from holding his weight and he soaked me in with his eyes before pushing himself off the bed.

"Soon. We can't afford the risk right now." He moved to the door and threw my jeans at the bed. "Come on. Up. We gotta get there before dawn."

Still half asleep, I dragged myself through the morning basics and before long, we were in the truck on our way back to the clearing. The headlights cut through the thick early mist, causing it to swirl past us as it danced across the truck.

As we pulled up along the old church at Doona, the crunch of the tires was enough to wake the dead. We parked beside Paul's car.

"Figures," Ryan stated, eyeballing the car.

We clicked on our flashlights and hiked the hills toward the clearing in pensive silence, wondering what each step closer might bring. Returning to the tomb was scary enough, but the thought of interpreting ancient rituals and dabbling in the magic of the Druids was enough to make me puke.

Then there was the memory of the eerie cry for help. Had I really heard it or was it just the wind moving through the spaces between the boulders, twisting into a sound that my mind thought it understood? I inhaled deeply to cleanse away my rising angst.

Entering the clearing, I saw Paul crouched over his bag of supplies with a lantern illuminating his work area.

"Mornin'," I called to him.

His head popped up and he squinted into our light beams.

"Mornin'," he called back. "Come and get geared up. We don't have much time before the sun's up."

I looked around the clearing and moved my light along the boulders.

"Where's Murt?" I asked.

Paul stood, fixing his tool belt to his waist. "He's not coming."

My shoulders settled in relief.

"Why not?" Ryan asked.

"Let's just say we have differing opinions on how to proceed with this site." He clipped a brush onto his belt. "I probably shouldn't have brought him in the first place. I just had no idea the gravity of what we would find. The possibilities." He pressed his vest pocket, probably to check for his glucose tabs. "He just wouldn't understand."

I nodded in agreement.

Before long, we were navigating the slick, narrow passageway toward the Keepers. My headlamp led the way and I moved with greater confidence this time, finding my footholds more easily from memory.

We regrouped at the Keepers before moving into the tunnel and through to the catacomb.

Paul looked at his watch. "In a few moments, dawn will break. We can see if any of its light enters the chamber. If it does, that will be evidence that a beam might line up at the solstice." He looked into the face of one of the Keepers. "If it's true, the beam might tell us something or lead to something. We'll have to be prepared for it."

Goosebumps lifted on my thighs and upper arms.

As I took my first step beyond the Keepers, a flutter of motion caught my attention. I shot my headlamp in its direction but missed it. It was the same motion that I'd noticed the first time we entered this space and it gave me a sick feeling in my gut, like we were being watched.

We moved through the large tunnel that led to the chamber as the sound of our footsteps mixed with the echoes of dripping water and the lonely depths of middle earth.

As we entered the catacomb, our lamps lit the space with an ethereal glow. The light bounced off all the walls, awakening the space that typically existed in pure darkness. A scraping sound of shifting gravel moved to us from the altar and we froze, angling our three beams in its exact direction.

"Who's there?" I called out.

We moved together around the altar and shone our lights behind it. A figure in a brown cloak cowered there, then stood with confidence. I stepped back as my breath surged in and out of me.

He stepped closer to our beams of light, as if unafraid of who we were or why we were there. Ryan's arm shot out in front of me, motioning for me to stay behind him. And then, in a slow, languid motion, the man reached for his hood and pulled it back off his head.

"You shouldn't be tampering with the sacred space of the Druids," Murt stated in a tone that shot fear through me.

"What the hell?" Paul choked, staring at Murt's robe. "I told you to stay off this site."

"The ancient order," Murt said. "We are this close to understanding time." He made the size of an inch with his thumb and forefinger. "And this is where the answers lie. I won't be kept from it."

My spine straightened at the sight of Murt in the robe of a Druid. And his strange intentions frightened me even more. He had said something about an ancient order and understanding time, which stirred a sinister panic in my gut.

"Yer out of line, Murt." Paul spoke through clenched teeth. "I told you not to come back here. It's not your place." He stepped closer to Murt, towering over him by several inches. "We've work to do now. Get out," he commanded.

"Oh, this *is* my place," Murt grumbled. "It has been for longer than you know." He pushed his chest out. "And not a chance I'm leavin' it. I've a duty to the order."

"What are you talking about?" My voice cracked; it was like Murt was a complete stranger. Or worse, an enemy. "We don't have time for games. Dawn is about to break. Just stop, we need to pay attention."

The last thing I wanted was for Murt to witness dawn's light with us here in the catacomb. But it was too late. The time was upon us and we couldn't afford to miss it. Still, my gut gnawed at me. It should all be protected from his greed and his strange behaviors.

"Step back to the side walls," Paul instructed. "If any light enters, it will likely hit the altar."

We clicked off our headlamps and stood in silence, three of us on one side, Murt on the other. The sound of my breathing filled the space around me and I was sure the others could hear my heart pounding.

Paul lit up his watch for one last time check. "Any moment now," he whispered.

Thirty seconds later a subtle glow grew at the top side of the chamber. A minuscule slit between two stones allowed the passage of dawn's first light. It sent a scattering of soft beams toward the small doors along the side near Murt.

One door in particular glowed in the light, widening Murt's eyes.

A moment later, the light faded and we were left again in complete darkness.

~

We clicked our lamps on and exploded with excitement, all of our voices mixing together with theories and ideas.

"The light of dawn entered the chamber!" I exclaimed, hardly believing my eyes. "The light of the solstice will be even more clear to guide us. I'm sure of it," I burst out with an energy I couldn't suppress.

"It's definitely encouraging," Paul stated, sending a narrow-eyed glare at Murt.

Murt stood in silence, staring at the door that had been illuminated by dawn's light.

Paul moved through the catacomb, taking pictures of ancient carvings and the medieval symbols and words on the altar.

"Don't disturb a thing," he said. Then leaned to me and whispered, "Now, we plan for the solstice." He stepped toward the tunnel and turned back again as Murt ran his hand over the small door that had been illuminated. "Murt. Move. Now."

Ryan and I squeezed out of the narrow passage first and hovered at the boulders waiting for Paul and Murt. After several moments, I crawled to the opening and called down, "Paul?"

The sound of kicking and slamming drifted up from the narrow passage and then their voices burst out of it.

"You're a liar and a thief," Paul shouted.

Then another slam.

"The ancient order holds more power than any of your arrogant degrees, McGratt. Time for you to walk away." Murt's voice poisoned the air.

More rustling and banging of equipment against the walls.

"Stop!" I shouted into the darkness. "I'm coming down there!"

I wiggled my legs into the passageway.

"No," Ryan shouted. "You'll get hurt. Let them work it out their way."

I looked back at him with bewilderment and then caught a glimpse of another brown cloak. In the clearing!

"Shit!" I pointed to the figure and Ryan turned to it.

"What the fuck," Ryan whispered, signaling for me to come closer to him.

I shimmied away from the hole and hunkered by him.

"Who the hell is that?" I said.

Then I called out, "Who are you? What are you doing here?"

The figure hovered, then moved to the far side of the clearing as the dark cloak billowed in the gusts from the sea.

We crawled out from the shelter of the boulders and moved into the center of the clearing.

"What do you want?" I moved closer to the cloaked person, who seemed to cower from the interrogation.

"I've come to protect the sanctuary of the Ovates." The grainy voice shook. "You don't understand its power. It will consume you."

I stepped closer and Ryan stood tall in surprise at the words and their familiar sound.

We approached the cloaked figure and I asked again, "Who are you?"

A wrinkled hand reached up from its oversized sleeve and pulled the hood until it fell back fully.

My hand flew to my mouth in shock and Ryan reeled back as his jaw dropped.

"Shanny?" he cried.

Maureen pulled the hood back up over her head and waved us closer. I hurried through the center of the clearing over to her and Ryan followed with disbelief plastered across his face.

"Ya see now," she started. "I'm a seer. Have been as long as I can remember and with that comes responsibility and obligation." She nodded at Ryan. "A duty to the Ovates." She paused. "And it's time ye knew, I'm supreme chief of the order."

Ryan moved past me to get closer to Maureen, as if to get a better look at her. "What do you mean?" He turned back to me. "What does that mean?"

"It's okay, Ryan," Maureen stated with a steady voice. "The danger lies in the disruption of the balance. Those with foul intentions can shift the delicate vibrations that hum through every flash of consciousness." She turned to me. "My purpose is to protect the Order of the Ovates—the Druid seers. And more specifically, the one who holds the power to end the curse. The seer of truth."

I exhaled the air I'd held since she first removed her hood. I'd read about the truth seer in the book of Druids. If Maureen knew of them as well, it had to be true. And therefore, it was critical that I find them. I would need their help to end all of this.

I looked to her with a new level of respect. One that went deeper than anything I could have ever known. Thank god she wasn't on the side of those who set the curse in motion. It was clear now she was on the good side. Our side.

"What is your intention, Isobel?" she asked.

I choked on my spit and coughed. Regaining composure, I pushed my defensiveness aside and focused on my mission.

"The summer solstice," I explained. "It's sacred to the Druids. I think it will lead me to answers about our visions and and how we can break the curse."

She nodded and listened.

I added, "I also think whatever we learn from the solstice, the rebirth, will help reconnect me to Maeve. She was dying last time I saw her and needed my help." My heart rate quickened at the thought of what we might learn that would have the power to release the secret of the seers. "It might be foolish to try, but I think if I connect with Maeve, it could be the force that reconnects the past with the present." I huffed at the insanity of my own words, then added, "It's worth an attempt."

Maureen stepped closer and reached for my hands. She held them in hers and spoke. "Your intentions are just. It *is* worth a try." She looked up into the air above the clearing. "So why do I sense disruption and foul intentions?"

Just as her question hit the open air, Paul pushed Murt out of the crevice with a loud grunt. "Yer a stubborn fucker," Paul said as he wiggled himself out as well. "Ya won't be opening that crypt any time soon. Not while I'm on site. We've no idea of what we might be disturbing."

"And you're a goddamn control freak," Murt barked back. "Too focused on your flippin' work and research methods. No surprise Patricia left, ya bastard."

It was like Paul took a bullet, the way his face grimaced from Murt's stinging words.

"Fuck you, Murt," he murmured.

Murt stood up and stumbled into the clearing. He wiped blood from his lip and then sweat from his forehead. As soon as he focused, he stared at the cloaked person and powered toward us.

"Who the hell are you?" he shouted past us as he barreled forward.

Ryan blocked him like a wall and Murt's smaller frame smacked right into his chest and bounced back.

"She's with us," Ryan stated, keeping Maureen behind him.

"It's okay, Ryan. I must confront him," she said. "I can feel it now. He is the disruption."

"Who sent you?" Murt blasted.

"I am of the Order of the Ovates," Maureen stated with steady tone. "And I'm here to protect the sacred house of worship of the Druids."

Murt let out an arrogant laugh.

"And I am of the Secret Society of Druids and am not to yield to your order." He looked down on her.

"Ach, yer nothin' but a rogue group of misfits," she fired back. "Spendin' centuries trying to control the Ovates and garnering their secrets for your own twisted purposes."

Murt stepped closer, into her personal space. "Since when is transcending time a twisted purpose? I'd call it a supreme calling, now wouldn't you?" he whispered as he passed by her.

Ryan lurched toward Murt and Maureen put her arm up to hold him back.

"And this exploitation, to what means?" Maureen pressed at Murt, causing him to turn back to her with a snarl.

"Are ya daft?" he shot back at her. "Harnessing time, of course. It's been the primary goal of the Druids for thousands of years. Predicting the future. Time travel."

Paul walked up behind us to hear better and I watched his face contort at Murt's maniacal words.

"Jesus, Murt. Have ya lost yer mind?" Paul blasted with a guffaw.

Maureen's eyes darted to Ryan's and mine and she nodded, assuring us that what Murt said was in alignment with what she understood of his rogue society.

Murt spun around to confront Paul again and their angry words flew at each other.

Maureen whispered to Ryan and me, "He must not be granted access on the solstice. He must be stopped at all costs. His intention is to steal the secrets of the seers and twist them for greed."

It made sense now.

I'd thought at first Murt was looking for treasure and museum items to make him famous. But it was bigger than that. What he was aiming to do for his secret society was extremist and crazy dangerous if it placed sacred Druid knowledge into the wrong hands.

"Is there anyone who can help us stop him while we're down there?" I asked. "As chief, or supreme chief, can you get us help?"

I hoped her position within the order held some form of power that could derail Murt from disrupting our mission. We had to do anything to keep him out during the solstice but, besides tying him up, I had no idea how he could be stopped.

"There is one I could ask," Maureen said. "The local chieftain of a most powerful clan. The clan that Murt aligns himself with." She pulled her hood tighter around her face in thought. "The chieftain has experienced the gift of the seers first hand. He understands. He would help us get Murt to stand down."

"Who is it, Shan?" Ryan pulled his headlamp off.

"The chieftain of the MacMahon clan," she stated. "I think you've met him on occasion. He's quite prominent in town. Known as Red King."

My air sucked in. I knew him.

"The guitar player?" Ryan coughed.

Maureen smirked. "Yes, dear. The guitar player. And chieftain to his clan." Her tone judged him for his superficial knowledge of such a powerful figure.

And then she added, "His name is Rory."

A surge ran through me and my mind burst with excitement from the sound of his name.

A name I hadn't heard in a very long time.

CHAPTER 13

I couldn't believe Maureen knew Rory. I stared at her in bewilderment. But it was Ryan who seemed even more stunned.

He studied Maureen's every movement, as if he didn't know her. I glimpsed moments of the awkward interactions between them as I continued to carve a map of the catacombs into the beach sand. I looked back over my shoulder—Doona Castle rose above the coast. My eyes wandered up the green hills back toward the clearing.

Then, just behind a crest, a motorbike revved along a ridge, cutting the tranquility with its high-pitched engine. Murt hunched at the handle bars and rode the rough terrain with effortless agility. Paul had pulled his car out and left a bit earlier and I could only imagine that they'd be meeting up again for round two, probably at the university.

It would be impossible to stop Murt from returning and disturbing the sanctity of the site but Paul seemed to think he might have a professional hold of ethics over him. Something told me, though, that discovering the secrets of time would trump any threats of tarnishing Murt's professional reputation.

"Ach, would ya stop gawking at me like that, Ryan." Maureen swatted at him. "I'm no different than when we had tea last night."

My attention shot back to Maureen and Ryan.

"But the feckin' robe, Shanny?" He shook his head.

Her shoulders squared. "It's the sacred cloak of the Druids, grandson. And ya might start gettin' used to it."

She stepped closer to my makeshift map and cocked her head to get perspective.

She continued to Ryan, "It's time ya knew yer full lineage, boy. We are seers, as you know. Ovates. And we too are Keepers of the Ovate Guard."

Ryan pushed off the rock where he'd been sitting and paced. "What do you mean 'we'?"

"Training of the Druids happens 'round yer age, Ryan. It just might have ta happen a little more quickly for you, considering the task you're entering into. We've no time to waste now."

Ryan chucked his jacket back at the rock and walked around my sketch. Maureen just watched him, allowing it to sink in.

I surprised myself with my own comfort in the situation of him becoming a Druid. It made perfect sense to me. I smiled inside as I pictured Ryan in a brown cloak. My blush proved he would make it hot, and plus, it was a noble thing, to carry forward thousands of years of worshipping the earth and its magical realms.

"I want to be trained too." I sat up taller and watched Maureen for a reaction. "Is it possible for me to become a Druid too?"

Maureen grinned. "Sure, you already are, dear. Don't ya feel it? Natural selection. Ya just need some fine tuning now, is all."

My eyes widened in wonder at the idea of being part of something larger than me. Something ancient and mystical. There was more to my visions than just being a freak.

I was a seer.

An Ovate.

And we were all descended from the Druid Ovates. Every seer had a connection to them and it would be up to each one how they used their gift.

I stared into the salty air as my purest form revealed itself to me. I would use my gift with the best intentions for those around me, always.

After several minutes of walking and throwing stones out to sea, Ryan finally came back and sat with Maureen again. His open demeanor proved he was ready for more now.

"The spiritual and magical training of a Druid begins with rebirth. Candidates for initiation must crawl into the cave of darkness to be reborn into the light of day," she described. "It's the process of death and rebirth that transcends you." Her eyes moved from him to me.

Ryan looked at me in surprise, likely realizing he wasn't the only Druid-in-training.

"Ya'll each go through the initiation. On yer own," she added. "Once ya emerge a true Druid, you'll have a better chance at facin' yer enemy." She glanced at each of us. "And it must be done immediately in preparation for the solstice. Best ya be equipped with full knowledge of Druidry before confronting the detractors of the order." She stood and straightened her cloak. "Now, cup a tea anyone?"

I chuckled at the simplicity of tea in such a complex moment as we headed back to the cars. But Maureen's jitters didn't go unnoticed by me. I sensed her anxiety in her fidgets and felt the same pressures of the looming solstice. The celestial event of the longest day of the year rushed the process of initiation for us, creating a stressful countdown we weren't quite ready for.

Maureen likely knew the ritual of rebirth into Druidry would happen for us at some point, but now, the clock was ticking and the idea of uncovering something so big, so fundamental to our existence, was mind blowing.

"I don't understand why we need to do this rebirth, before the solstice. What's the rush?" Ryan asked.

I slowed to hear her response.

"Like I said before, without full understanding of the power of the Druids, it will consume you. You would be lost to us."

I shot a glance to Ryan and his eyes met mine with similar concern.

~

Maureen had parked her compact car next to Ryan's truck, probably when we were in the catacomb, and I couldn't help but wonder what other secrets she held—like her unexpected connection to Rory. We climbed into our vehicles to head back to the cottage.

She was right though. Rory had experienced the visions of the past with Maeve and he saw their power in action. He had been haunted by them actually, but he'd still attempted to travel with her through the portal, only to be ripped away at the last minute and left behind.

But now, it seemed he'd become known for his involvement in the mystical encounters. His ability to engage in Maeve's visions and then have his own...My racing mind stopped short. Could Rory be a Druid too? An Ovate? My breath paused as I contemplated the notion, rolling it over in every direction in my head.

If Rory were to get involved now, alongside Paul—the two men who had vied for Maeve's affections--there was no telling what might happen.

~

After settling in back at the cottage, I'd become so engrossed in reading intricate details of sacrificial rituals and annual worship rites in the *Ancient Book of Druids,* I hadn't even noticed the knock at the door. It was only when Maureen shook my shoulder and pushed me back toward Ryan's room that I realized our safety was compromised.

As I flew into Ryan's room, I looked back and saw Mrs. Flannery's profile pressing into the front window for a look inside. My heartbeat shot into my throat as I prayed she hadn't seen me.

"Anybody home?" she called from the front stoop. "Ya can't avoid people forever, you know."

Maureen's sigh filled the cottage.

"What the hell does she want?" Ryan snapped. "We don't have time for her bullshit right now."

My foot tapped in anticipation of her calculated agenda and I peeked through a narrow crack in the door.

"I suppose we'll just have to see." Maureen pulled the door open and filled the space to be sure Mrs. Flannery didn't invite herself in. "Good day, Mrs. Flannery." Maureen's tone held no friendship and barely any civility.

"How ya, Maureen," she said with a nod. "Ryan."

I watched her poke her eyes around the cottage, trying to nudge past Maureen, and I squeezed the door shut in fear of being detected.

"What can I do for you? We're quite busy right now," Maureen pressed.

"Oh. Well, fine. Sure, I thought there was always time for a cuppa tea," Mrs. Flannery pressured Maureen.

"Ah sure, not today. Sorry. Have a fine day fer yourself, now." And the creak of the door closing made me chuckle.

"Oh, one more thing," Mrs. Flannery added. "Ya see, there's more news. Of Isobel."

"I told you we're busy. Now good day." The creak grew louder along with the speed of the closing door.

The thud must have been Mrs. Flannery's foot stopping the door from closing. I struggled to hear through the pounding of my heart in my ears.

"There's been no body found, ya see. There's talk that she might not have met the gruesome demise that horrified us all." Her fake words of concern made my stomach turn, but the message caused the blood to drain from my head.

I stumbled back onto Ryan's bed and dropped my head between my knees.

If there was talk of no body being found, then surely suspicion was growing that I was a runaway.

"We'll not be needin' updates from the likes of you, Mrs. Flannery. Now kindly remove your foot before I close the door on it," Maureen commanded.

"No need ta get pissy. I'm just tryin' ta..."

Slam.

Maureen's and Ryan's voices filled the cottage, first with rage and then systematic planning.

"Stay put, Isobel. No telling how long she'll lurk," Maureen whispered through the door.

I rocked on Ryan's bed, feeling powerless before that woman's efforts at stopping me. If anything, her hunt fueled my purpose and drove me to accomplish it faster.

It was time for my rebirth. Time to go through the formal initiation into the order of the Druids.

Once I reached that level, I was sure I would have a stronger ability to end the curse set by the deviant sector. The book was clear in stating special abilities belonging to those within the Druid order. If I could pass the initiation into that order, I had no doubt it would strengthen my ability to use my visions to their highest degree...and ultimately, have the power to save Maeve and end the curse.

If I could achieve that transcendental goal, it could resound through time, all the way to my present moment. It might even be enough to redirect the witch hunt in my daily life. If the curse was over, then maybe Mrs. Flannery and Sister Margaret might lose interest and get off my tail.

Maybe.

What I was sure of, though, was that it needed to happen now. Every second mattered. And the moment of the solstice couldn't be missed or it would be all over.

I creaked Ryan's door open and poked my head out.

"It's time," I said.

Maureen and Ryan lifted their heads from the book and stared at me.

"No. It's too soon. She might still be out there at the hedges," Ryan said.

"No. I mean it's time for our initiations. We can't delay any longer."

Maureen and I waited in the clearing for Ryan to emerge from the dark passageway. My diplomatic coin toss for who would go first bit me in the ass when he called tails. I didn't know what was scarier, going first or being the one to have to wait and then witness the emergence of the frazzled newly initiated. Going first seemed like the better deal.

Ryan, however, had fought to go first to be sure it was safe, and gloated after winning the toss. But I assumed our experiences in the catacombs would be vastly different, considering my connection to Maeve and the nature of my visions, so in the end, it didn't matter.

"Six hours in the hole will feel like an eternity," Maureen said. "Not much longer now though." She tapped on her watch.

We'd sent Ryan down the gloomy passage at dusk, around 11:00pm, knowing that sunrise would be a bit after 5:00am. He went down without any gear, including no flashlight. The point was pure solitude in complete darkness within the chamber with the altar.

Once dawn broke and shone its first light through, he could emerge. It would be his rebirth.

Maureen and I leaned against the boulders with our blankets wrapped over our shoulders. We may have each dozed off once or twice, but for the most part it was an all-nighter.

Before long, the miracle of first light hit. I hopped to my feet in anticipation then reached for Maureen's hand and helped pull her up to standing. We stared into each other's eyes, waiting, wondering, and then his voice tore at us.

His screams ripped at our souls and we ran to the opening of the passageway. I inhaled, preparing to yell his name, and Maureen pressed her hand to my mouth.

"No. It's all a part of it. Let him work through it." She nodded as she removed her hand.

His screams travelled up through the narrow opening and filled the clearing with his pain and suffering.

"He's hurt!" I pressed my face closer to the passageway. "He needs help."

"Step back now, Isobel. We need to give him space to emerge into the light of day." Her tone remained steady.

My shaking hands pushed my hair out of my face as my entire

body trembled in fear. What could he be going through that would cause him such anguish? I couldn't stand it for another second.

"I hear him. He's moving up through the passage now." Maureen lifted a finger to her lips. "Let's give him plenty of room."

We moved to the middle of the clearing and stared at the crevice for any sign of Ryan. Dawn's light glowed on the hills and illuminated everything around us in a magical hue of gold. And then his hand reached out from the darkness and pulled the rest of him from the narrow crevice.

He crawled out of the boulders and pressed up against one of them. Maureen went to him and wrapped her blanket around his shoulders, then stepped back with me.

He rocked and then he wept.

Maureen kept her arm around me to prevent me from going to him. His despair ripped at my heart and the need to console him tore at me.

After what must have been at least an hour, he finally lifted his head and looked at both of us. He nodded at Maureen as if to acknowledge that it was done, his transformation.

And then his eyes locked onto mine and a sinister grin pulled the sides of his mouth into a spine-chilling sneer.

Ryan didn't speak the entire ride home and I had picked my cuticles raw by the time we got there. Maureen insisted on sleep to prepare for my initiation this evening but there was no chance of slumber in my near future. I was too wound up by Ryan's freak out.

It was like his mind had been blown and the pieces were still lost on the wind.

His sneer, though. It curdled my blood. Almost like something evil had entered him or twisted his mind somehow. I glanced at him any chance I got, attempting to see him as the Ryan I always knew. But he was different.

I prayed that wouldn't happen to me and that he would go back to normal. Maybe the terror of the experience just needed to fade before he could be strong again.

There wasn't enough time for complications like this, though. There was too much I needed to accomplish in these final days leading to the solstice. If I had a brain of mush or worse, a battle between good and evil happening inside me like what Ryan seemed to be going through, I'd be useless to the entire mission.

What did he experience down there anyway? What could he have seen that would make him react like that?

I flipped through the book again and after seeing the image of a dagger ripping through a man's chest while others read the spilled blood in an attempt to predict the future, I slammed the book shut.

"It's all quite normal, dear." Maureen placed a cup of tea in front of me. "I've seen it before. I don't fear for Ryan. He'll be stronger and wiser when he comes out of this."

But I liked him the way he'd been before. Stronger and wiser might cause him to change his path or become a different person. A nagging insecurity chewed at my gut. Was I losing him?

"How much longer before he, you know, snaps out of it?" I asked.

"No telling. Typically, a few hours. I expect he'll be fit ta come with us tonight for your initiation," she said.

I wondered if I even wanted him there now. It was like he was unpredictable at the moment. Like I wasn't even sure who he was yet.

"Go on. Take yer cuppa and have a lie down." Maureen carried my tea as she encouraged me to follow her to Ryan's room.

I complied and laid my head on his pillow but my eyes refused to close even a slight amount. My internal disturbance blurred between concern for Ryan and churning panic for my own rite of initiation.

As the minutes crawled by like hours, I felt like jumping out of my skin and hopped up. Just as I opened the bedroom door, their voices wafted in around me.

Ryan and Maureen talked by the fire and as soon as I popped my head out, they stopped.

I looked at Ryan and caught a glimpse of the sparkle returning to his eyes. Ever since my escape from the island, I had been searching for that sparkle and worried that it had faded forever. But here it was again.

"Hi," he said.

My eyes shot wide. "Hi," I said back and stepped out of his room.

"Sorry if I freaked you out." He walked over to me. "It was a little intense. I should probably prepare you a bit before you go down."

Relief poured over me like warm honey. He seemed normal again.

"Huh, yeah. No," I stumbled on my words. "I mean, I should probably go down with a clear, open mind."

Maureen interjected, "She's right, Ryan. Ya shouldn't set any expectations for her. Her experience will be quite different from yers, anyhow."

"Yeah, but at least I should warn her of the…"

"No." Maureen cut him off. "She'll be fine."

CHAPTER 14

If I hadn't witnessed Ryan's violent rebirth, I wouldn't be shaking out of my skin on the way to my own. Why the hell did I need to be reborn anyway? Just because it was a thousands-of-years-old ritual of the ancient Druid Order, to which I desperately wanted to belong?

Argh.

My angst clouded my reason. The rebirth would empower me with a direct connection to the magic of the Druids. It would open me to be able to access fully the mysticism of their society. I always had it within me, but the process of the initiation would allow me to make the full connection to my abilities.

And this was what scared me.

I had no idea who I would become or how it would change me.

And the level of responsibility to my order, as the one who could make contact with Maeve in the past and actually influence a bridge through time--it couldn't be denied.

I really shouldn't have had so much tea before we left the cottage. It added jittery layers to my shaking nerves. I picked at my nails then fidgeted with the cinch sack on my lap.

"You okay?" Ryan leaned toward me and rested one hand on my bag.

I gazed into my side mirror to be sure Maureen was still close behind.

"I guess." I swallowed hard. "I mean, it *is* the first time I've ever participated in an ancient ritual. Kind of a big deal."

He chuckled. "Yeah. Kinda."

As we entered Ballycroy, I shifted in my seat, preparing myself for a quick descent into the abyss of doom. It was already 10:30pm and I knew I'd have to disappear into the darkness by 11:00. Dusk to dawn, basically.

The thought of making my way through the narrow passage and past the guardians in the pitch dark, guided by sense of touch alone, was terrifying. Then I'd have to feel my way through the tunnel that led to the chamber with the altar. At that point, I'd be so freaked out I'd probably try to hide in a corner or something, waiting to be taken by goblins or tortured by cave trolls.

But the rational side of me, whatever was left of it, feared my own mind. I'd read about what solitary confinement could do to prisoners of war. They'd go mad. Their own thoughts would spiral to the point where they could no longer tell reality from hallucinations.

This was what I had to prepare myself for. And I was sure it was what Ryan experienced too.

"I feel like I need to warn you about something," Ryan said out of the blue.

"Okay..."

"Maureen didn't think I should, but I don't know." He hesitated. "It's just that..."

"No. Ryan." I stopped him. "I trust Maureen. She knows how this works. Please. Wait to tell me when I come out. And of course, if this is the wrong decision, I'll beat you, hard, for not telling me now." I chuckled.

He pulled the truck in by the ancient church ruin.

"We'll have to head up without Maureen. She'll be too slow on the climb." He waved for her to park next to us. She had been showing signs of exhaustion back at the cottage and her slump proved she'd reached her limit. "I'll come back down for her once you are all set."

"Wait, you can't leave me in there." My voice cracked. "Ryan?"

"You're right. Shit. Hang on."

He helped Maureen out of her car and hoisted her bag onto his back.

"You alright for the trek in the hills, Shan?" he asked her.

"Fit as a fiddle, lad." She smacked him on the ear. "Let's get climbing."

Her feet dragged in the gravel and she struggled to see past her heavy lids, but her spirit kept her moving.

Ryan threw his own pack over Maureen's on his back and nodded for me to go first.

My cinch sack had simple basics like water and a flashlight, but its comforts would sit waiting for me in the clearing while I went caving without supplies. Ryan assured me my fleece would be enough to keep me warm. My adrenaline and racing heart would take care of the rest.

Maureen lumbered along the beginning of the trail, and I worried about her health. She was pushing herself too hard.

"I think I'll walk up ahead to get a feel for the clearing before I actually have to go down," I called back to them.

"Sure, go on. I'll catch up," Maureen agreed.

Ryan shifted between the two of us, torn as to who he should stay with, and I assured him with a nod that it was Maureen.

My legs carried me the rest of the way up the trail without a single moan of resistance and with my excess energy I lapped around the inner perimeter of the clearing a couple times. Checking my phone for the time, I shook it when the dead screen offered no response, even with a full charge.

I was sure it was nearly 11:00pm though. I'd need to begin my descent shortly and couldn't risk losing any time.

Dusk to dawn.

That was the expectation.

I moved to the edge of the clearing and looked down to check on their progress. Ryan signaled for me to wait another minute and began to jog. Before long, he'd made it up to where I was, panting.

"She's a bit slow and shaky on her feet. As long as I can see her, we're good." He glanced back and waved. "I was hoping for a more formal send off. I'm sorry it's so rushed."

"It's okay. But I think it makes sense for me to go down now. Promise me you won't leave me." My eyes begged his.

"I promise, Isobel. With all my heart."

I reached for him for a final embrace, not knowing what I would be like upon my return, but just as my hands grazed his shoulders he pulled away.

"No. You'll see too much," he said. "My mind is ablaze with everything from the cave. Wait until you come out."

I ached to have him hold me. And I worried about what he had tried to tell me earlier.

"Okay. You're right." I stepped toward the boulders that protected the passageway. Crouching onto my knees, I looked back and Ryan waved one last time.

Then I shimmied my way into the opening to the vast darkness below.

~

Though already dusk in the clearing, nothing could have prepared me for the profound darkness I entered deep in the earth. Unable to make out even the simplest of shapes, I closed my eyes to protect them from unseen harm. In the same instant, my ears took over as my primary sense. My perception of touch led me down the narrow, slick passage.

I moved down along the rocks with surprising ease as my body remembered the intricacies of each step. Without hesitation or even caution, I made it around the bend and to the feet of the Keepers of the Ovate Guard.

"Hi," I whispered as my hands moved along the shins of the closest guardian.

I stepped up onto his feet and reached higher toward his massive head. My hands explored his face and my fingers moved around his huge eyes. I climbed down from him and moved to the second one. I found his hand and identified each of his fingers and then climbed toward his face as well. For some reason, I examined his eyes too and then felt safe enough to move forward into the tunnel.

That was weird, I thought. Like I needed to connect with them somehow, for safety maybe.

But in truth, it wasn't strange. It hadn't felt weird at all. It actually felt like an appropriate greeting to old friends. Protectors. In fact, that reunion process was very similar to how a blind person would greet someone they were close with.

And maybe taking the time to understand what was around me would help me to see better.

I stepped forward into the tunnel and moved through it without hesitation. It was only when I reached the chamber that I realized I hadn't been using my hands as my guide at all. I was following my sense of direction and intuition, and they were sharply accurate.

Moving into the chamber, I walked forward until I hit the altar. I'd arrived at my destination and now had approximately five and a half hours to kill. I probably should have taken longer to get here but it was just too easy to navigate the maze and my nervous energy had kept me moving fast.

I ran my hands along the top of the altar, feeling every divot and imperfection on its surface, and then ran them along the sides. The carvings generated pictures in my mind and the more I traced them the faster the images moved. I circled around the altar, keeping my hands in full contact with the carvings as an old movie played out in my mind of ancient Druids, sacred rituals, and then, specific plans.

Step by step instructions. Like how to construct something.

I stopped and the movie playing in my mind stopped with me.

Oh my god. Paul had no idea of the level of information that was contained within these carvings. I shuddered at the idea of being able to decipher the plans more than him, piecing together thousands of years of Druid knowledge.

I stood and listened to my rhythmic breathing. It was the only sound, the only anything, that existed in this sacred space.

And then more breathing.

My heart stopped.

No, that would be crazy. I was the only one here. It was just the sound of my own breath bouncing off the walls of this deep space. I repeated the explanation over and over as the sound of the other breathing grew closer.

It was only when I realized I was holding my own breath that pure terror washed over me. I crouched at the altar to hide.

Then a soft glow tickled my lids, opening my eyes. Gentle light flickered off the walls, just barely illuminating the catacombs.

"Murt?" I whispered.

No reply.

I used whatever muscles would cooperate to lift my eyes over the top of the altar.

I stumbled back from the sheer force of my gasp that was so long and so loud, it embarrassed me even in the moment of my own possible death.

Staring across the altar at me was an old man, wrinkled from time but with light in his eyes. He lifted his cloaked arm and a metal pan swung from a chain in his hand as its glowing coals lit the area more.

"Who are you?" I sobbed. Terror had stolen all of my composure and I struggled to even speak.

"I am Desmond. The Keeper of the Ovate Guard." His voice held a gentle tone.

"Wh...what?" I kicked at the floor, pressing back, in hopes I could disappear into the wall.

"I am Desmond. Protector of this sacred crypt. I wait for the truth seer. Are you she?" He stepped closer and I nearly lost continence.

"I, I'm Isobel." My voice shook as tears rolled down my face.

"What brings you here, child?" he asked as his pan of glowing coal swung back and forth.

"Umm," I swallowed. "I'm here for my initiation. My rebirth into the Order of the Druids." My voice shook without control.

He reached for the hood of his cloak and pulled it down. "Order of the Druids?"

"Yes, sir."

"What do you know of the Order?" he asked.

Pull yourself together, Isobel.

This had to be a vision. A hallucination. But he seemed so real. So alive.

His eyes glistened in the yellow glow.

His wrinkled skin told stories of the ages.

His swollen knuckles proved hard work and endurance.

"Well, I'm still learning." My courage returned with each new breath and the honesty in his eyes made me trust him. "I've had visions, all my life. They connect me to the past. And I want to learn how to use them properly. To help."

"Mm. I see, Isobel. You have the gift of the seers. And it's led you here, no?" He tipped his head.

He knew I was seer now. Maybe he was too. If he was even real. Maybe he could guide me on what to do next.

"I think, if I connect with the Order of the Druids…through their ritual of rebirth, I'll gain the ability to use my visions…for more."

"As a true Ovate," he stated.

"Yes." I hesitated. "Maybe it will take me to the level where I can put an end to an old curse that's been placed on the seers. A rift in time. Like it's been disconnected." My words began to sound more like rambles and I stifled myself.

He dangled his glowing pan closer to my face and gazed into my eyes. I fought the instinct to retract from his intense scrutiny and allowed him to see into me.

"I think you may be the one I've been waiting for, Isobel," he murmured. "I sense a pure heart in you. With good intention."

Waiting? The idea clamped my stomach, causing it to cramp.

"You've been…w-waiting?" I stammered.

How long?

Did Ryan meet him here last night? I couldn't be sure. But nobody could survive long down here in the cold and the damp. Particularly the elderly.

And I didn't even know I'd be coming here tonight until just a day or two ago.

"Yes. Waiting for some time now," he said. "The solstice will mark my stay here to the exact point that the Druids predicted your arrival." He inhaled. "And I've waited each day as the Keeper. To be sure we wouldn't miss you."

My breath stopped as I watched him lower his coal pan slightly.

Then he continued, "The solstice will mark, exactly, my five hundredth year of waiting."

~

The Immortal Druid.

It was the title of one of the chapters of Maureen's book. The picture of him in the pages looked nothing like Desmond but the idea was the same. And I recognized the coal pan from the book as well. It was an ancient-style lantern used by the Druids for thousands of years.

Either my mind was playing the most grandiose hoax of its entire consciousness or something truly mystical was happening down here. Considering I'd hardly had time to go insane from the isolation, I was leaning toward mystical.

"I must leave you in darkness, Isobel, for you to experience your rebirth." Desmond stepped back and moved to the other side of the altar.

"Wait. I have so many questions. Did you meet Ryan last night? What will happen to me here? Where will you go?" I pushed off the wall and moved closer to him as my questions flooded out of me.

"I have only revealed myself to you," he stated. "I knew it to be you the moment you first arrived and discovered this place. And now you've confirmed my premonition." He lowered his pan, returning darkness to the chamber, and then stepped further away from me. "I wait within the walls of the tomb, with its secrets and its truths." He motioned his head toward the wall.

How was that even possible? My mind exploded with the concept of the Keeper. But at the same time, he brought me courage, enough to move forward with my journey through the darkness.

“I don’t know what to do now.” My trembling voice begged him to stay.

"Keep your heart and your mind open. Allow the process to take you. And then at the solstice, if you are who you say, you will acquire enlightenment that only a poet could even begin to describe."

His words silenced me, shooting terror through my nerves.

I would be changed. Forever.

Was I ready for it?

I thought of everything I’d been through, every fear, every vision, and it was clear. I’d been preparing my whole life for this.

And I was ready.

"Wait, you called this place a tomb. Who is buried here?" I asked him.

"If you are the truth seer, you already know."

My hairs stood up on end and every nerve in my body tingled.

"Maeve." Her name choked through my lips.

"Yes. Maibh. Our Gaelic queen. Chieftain to the Clan O'Maille,” he said. “She had mastered the power of time itself, and many wanted to steal it from her."

My breathing quickened at the idea of standing in Maeve's final resting place. And the knowledge that she had even died. It overwhelmed my mind.

"How did she…die?" I leaned over the altar.

"'Twas a curse. Cast by the Secret Society of Druids, forever seeking to harness the power of time. Their curse caused her to fade until nothing was left at all."

I gasped, remembering her condition when I last saw her at Rockfleet. Fading. But I had hoped returning the ring to her would have reversed it.

But now, it was as if the curse accomplished its greater goal of stopping time, which therefore caused Maeve to fade completely. And maybe to have never even existed. But if this was her final place of rest, then that was proof that she existed.

I thought back to Maureen’s and the technologies that no longer existed. My useless cell phone. And I’d noticed the silent skies over the past week. No more planes filled the air with their rumbling engines and streaking white smoke trails. The curse was affecting progress which proved it had the power to turn time back on itself.

If Maeve faded to the point of never existing, then everything I knew and loved would suffer the same fate. Including me.

It became more critical than ever that I pull Maeve back to us.

"But she was so young," I murmured.

"Not so," Desmond corrected me. "She had the power of her ring to fight the curse. 'Twas only in her later years and failing health that the ring could no longer protect her."

My chest fell in relief that she had a full life at Rockfleet. I couldn't imagine what her lover's reaction to an early death would have been, though I was sure he'd suffered greatly from her loss even in their golden years.

But why didn't she use the ring to return to this time, to avoid her death? Instead she chose to spend her final days with him.

Desmond added, "Her death was mourned across the countryside, but the grief soon turned to a celebration of her life and her dedication to preserving Gaelic Ireland. Her legend will carry on forever in the mystical rhythms of the land." His eyes moved across the catacombs. "The solstice marks the five hundredth year since her passing."

Oh my god. The measure of time was bigger than my mind could comprehend. But from what Desmond said, Maeve had accomplished her mission. She'd stabilized Gaelic Ireland and was honored for her leadership and commitment to the Ovates.

I browsed the variety of doors and alcoves along the catacombs, wondering which one was hers.

"There was nothing left of her once she was gone. She faded, then absorbed into the cosmos, becoming one with the rhythms of nature and everything around us." He pressed his back against the far wall. "Her essence entered all of our souls that final day. And we gathered her treasures and laid them to rest here. And then the guard began."

As he leaned further into the wall, a crack formed around him and golden beams crept out from the seams. "Focus, young Isobel. On your rebirth. On Maibh's essence. And you will come to enlightenment."

And he was gone.

"Desmond!" I called out.

After a final bright flash, all hints of light fell silent and I was left in complete darkness. I gripped the edges of the altar to ensure my time and place as my mind swam with a million questions. My breath moved into me in gasps and I buckled to the floor, unable to stand any longer.

Curling into a fetal position, I rocked, lulling myself against the deprivation on my senses. The absence of light only amplified the onslaught to my brain and tears poured from my eyes, followed by full-body sobs.

My body twitched and jolted uncontrollably, causing me to sit up. I had no measure of time since Desmond left me, except for the amount of wetness on my face and neck. The collar of my fleece was soaked too, proving it had been more than a brief episode.

But now I stood and placed my hands back on the altar. With my feet squared solidly beneath me, I waited.

As I stared into blackness, my mind turned over and over on every word Desmond had spoken. His message carried more information than I'd realized at first and my understanding grew with each passing heartbeat—my only measure of time.

Then, as if a bulb went off, I gasped and fell back from the intensity of my understanding.

My first enlightenment.

My eyes widened as light filled my vision, confirming my reawakening. I followed the beams to their source high up on the ceiling.

Dawn.

And with the dawn came my new understanding. My rebirth.

Maeve had faded from Rockfleet, but she hadn't died. Instead she was now trapped in the abyss, somewhere between there and here.

She had faded into the cosmos in her launch back through time. Maybe the curse had made it impossible for her to make her return here or maybe she'd grown so weak she just lost her way.

But her visions held her somewhere in limbo.

And it was my new order to bring her back. To connect her past to the present.

To close the wormhole of time created by the curse and restore the balance of the Druids.

It was up to me.

I was the truth seer.

CHAPTER 15

I flew out of the chamber and through the dark tunnel toward the Keepers. I ran past them with a brief farewell of "I'll be back soon," and pushed my way up the narrow passage. Squirming along the final wedge of stones, I pressed myself into the cleansing light of dawn with a guttural grunt.

I lay at the opening, panting from exhaustion, and a helping hand reached down to me. I grabbed onto it and allowed his strength to pull me to standing. My wide-eyed elation quickly turned to closed-off defense as I stared into Murt's sinister face.

Words eluded me as they proved to be too simple of a form of communication in my heightened sense of enlightenment. Spoken language just wasn't enough to express what I had experienced. I had reached a new level of consciousness that blew my mind and even the site of Murt couldn't take that away from me.

Questions punched at the back of my mind—needing to know where Ryan and Maureen were, wondering if they were safe, and searching for an explanation for Murt's presence. But I couldn't snap out of the haze of my subterranean experience. It had opened my mind in a way that was more profound than anything else.

I released Murt's hand and leaned against a boulder, allowing myself to slide down it to a comfortable sitting position of contemplation. Beyond my control, the need to process my experience trumped everything else.

Then Murt started speaking but I didn't even register his words as I stared into the beauty of the clearing.

"What the mmph...did the mwahhhh..." His words morphed into strange sounds of insignificance in my head as I stared into the mist of morning.

Images of cloaked Druids whirled around a fire in worship to the cosmos. I smiled as I watched the ancient ritual celebrating nature—the true nature in us all. Their shadows danced along the boulders, filling the clearing with their honor of the universe.

I watched the ritual play out over a span of time. The faces of the Druids changed but the clearing remained the same as did the rhythm of their dance.

As the light of their fire and the mesmerizing flow of their movements faded, my head fell back in wonderment.

"Isobel?" Ryan's gentle voice coaxed me back to the moment.

I blinked and lifted my head.

Looking him in the eyes, I saw a stranger and pushed away from him. The punching at the back of my brain broke through and lucid consciousness returned like a tsunami.

"It's okay," he said. "It's just me."

I scanned the perimeter of the clearing, searching for Murt as my heart pounded out of my chest.

Something was wrong.

"Where's Maureen?" My voice scratched out of me.

"She's back at the car. She couldn't quite make the last legs of the trek up here." He motioned his head in the direction of the vehicles. "It was just too much for her, two nights in a row."

My eyes narrowed. I didn't believe him.

It was as if I could see right through him. He'd had an ulterior motive ever since his rebirth and his subtle attempts at derailing me were now blaring.

The sneer on his face when he returned from his rebirth, it played over and over in my mind. Like he saw me as an enemy. Something had shifted in him down in the hole, as if he had been turned against me somehow.

And now, I trusted not what my eyes and ears picked up on, but I trusted my truth sight.

And that intuition screamed defector.

He'd joined with Murt. He'd betrayed me. Betrayed Maureen. And the Order of the Ovates.

"You've turned to the Secret Society," I stated.

He stepped back like I'd slapped his face. But said nothing.

"Why?" I pressed.

He paced and ran his hands through his hair, pulling on it as if fighting his inner demons.

"The power of time travel, Isobel. I was so close to it down there. The answers were all around me." He stared into the darkness of the crevice. "Do you have any idea the power it holds?" His tone held condescension, like I was a simpleton, and my blood boiled.

Of all people, Ryan was the one who I thought would want nothing to do with this. He avoided his gift like the plague. But now, it had all shifted. Like he got a taste of power greater than any man's. And it had poisoned him.

Murt stepped out from behind the boulders and stood by Ryan.

"Ryan, no. Please." I begged him to return to me. "You're on the wrong path."

"We'll kindly ask ya ta tell us what you know." Murt stepped closer. "You can make this easy." He paused. "Or you can make it difficult."

My eyes darted back to Ryan's and he avoided contact, knowing I'd be able to read his intentions.

My heart broke in that moment as betrayal seethed through me. How could he do this? His intentions had always been so pure. Something happened to him in the chamber, I knew that. And now I had to wonder if it was controlling him, with some sort of voodoo that he couldn't break free from.

My only chance was to run but there was no way to outrun two grown-ass men. I side-stepped along the boulders to place a little more space between us and scanned the perimeter for my best chance at an exit from the clearing.

Just as my legs readied for flight, Murt grabbed onto my left arm and squeezed with a grip that only a true enemy would use. I reeled back with my right arm and with a clenched fist, I shot a clear punch directly to his nose. Blood burst from it and he buckled in pain with a grunt of disbelief.

I turned and ran as fast as my legs could carry me.

"Grab her, Ryan. Hold onto her and see everything she knows," Murt shouted.

Oh my god. He knew Ryan's gift.

My legs moved faster but Ryan still caught up to me without struggle. I turned and yelped as he reached for me and then I smacked right into someone else. The man's arms steadied me and then passed me behind him to a group of others.

"Don't even think about touching her or we'll beat the living shit out of you," Rory commanded.

My jaw dropped.

Rory had changed so much since I last saw him at the time of Maeve's disappearance. Over six years ago.

He was stronger now. More confident. Power and wisdom oozed from him.

I moved back into the safety of his clansmen.

"Colm, take her to Maureen," Rory ordered, "while the rest of us take care of Ryan and Murt here. There're some lessons to be taught. And some cleansing to accomplish."

I ran the entire way down the hillside with Colm just behind me. Once Maureen was in my sight, I relieved him of his duty and sent him back up to the clearing. His slow reluctance and backward gazes had made it obvious he didn't want to miss any more of the confrontation above.

Maureen lumbered toward me as I ran the rest of the distance between us. I threw my arms around her and we embraced with full strength, both hearts racing.

"Ryan's turned," she stated. "I saw it in his eyes. He's...distracted."

She knew.

And she sent Rory for back up.

"I know. It feels like betrayal, Maureen," I agreed. "But it's like something is controlling him. Something took over a part of him that was vulnerable. We'll get him back," I promised. "We have to."

She nodded with confidence in my words. I only wished I felt as confident inside. The shock of seeing him partnered with Murt was beginning to wear off and left a foul aftertaste of pain in my heart mixed with anger in my fists.

I lowered my eyes to avoid hers. To avoid the possible truth that maybe he had completely turned on us.

I couldn't imagine what held the power to shift him against everything we were working for, but it must have been strong. And would he really have grabbed me, the way Murt commanded him to? I didn't want to believe that he could but it sure seemed like he planned to follow orders, until he was stopped.

I pictured him running right into Rory and getting the shock of his life. That encounter was probably the last thing he expected. And Murt must have crapped his pants knowing Rory's position within the clan, and now being exposed in front of him.

"How did you get Rory here so fast?" My tone held awe at her power move.

She tapped the side of her head. "Intuition, dear. I followed my instincts," she said. "It's what we all relied upon before the connectivity of our mobile phones." She lifted her phone from her pocket and hit it a few times to see if it would come to life. "See, now that these things don't work anymore, no one knows how to function. Except me, of course."

I smiled and reached for my own phone to check and it, too, was still dead with a full charge.

"Ryan forgets I'm connected in other ways." And she let out a guffaw at her own techno-savvy pun. "Thinks I'm too old and out of touch. Bit him in the arse, it did."

My chuckle purged me of my tension and I grinned at Maureen.

She knew to go get reinforcements and Rory came through. She was a godsend. And Rory too. True guardians of the Ovates.

"Maureen." I hesitated and took a deep breath. "Something you mentioned before...What do you know of the truth seer?" I asked.

Her eyes widened.

"I knew it," she stated with a smirk.

Tires barely touching the pavement, Maureen flew through the narrow winding roads leading away from the mystical clearing in Ballycroy. My heart pounded in my ears, reminding me that this was now a race. A race against time, enemies, and the coming solstice.

"The university." My voice broke our intense focus. "I need to see Paul."

"Got it." Maureen took the exit for Galway City Centre.

For starters, Paul needed to know what Murt did, or tried to do. And Ryan.

I didn't want to tell him about Ryan. His betrayal caught in my throat, yet I still wanted to protect him.

I also needed to tell Paul about what I'd discovered about Maeve. That she might be caught in the abyss, needing to find her way back to us. The news would blow his mind, but it was what he'd been waiting all these years for. Her.

"What do you think they're doing to Ryan?" My thoughts continued to be distracted by the lost look in his eyes, his confusion when Rory intercepted his attack on me.

"I've given very strict instruction," Maureen started. "The boy must face his worst fear. Again. But this time, he must defeat it in order for it to release him."

"What do you mean?" I held my breath, envisioning a fierce beating or other form of abuse.

"They'll send him down into the hole again." She paused. "For much longer this time. Enough time to strip him of everything he is and rebuild him again."

“Oh my god,” I whispered, remembering his blood-curdling screams from the first time.

“His second rebirth will be grueling. Painful, even. But necessary," she added.

My air sucked in and I turned to look at the road behind us. I was tempted to go back for him, worried about what might happen. Would he fall apart under the strain?

"So we have until dawn, then?" I calculated what needed to be done between now and Ryan's reemergence.

Maureen swerved into the university gates.

"Right. A little less than twenty-four hours before we know who our true allies are," she said as I directed her toward Paul's building.

As I glanced up the enormous granite stairs leading to the musty, echoing halls that wove to his office, one of the heavy entryway doors flew open.

"Shit!" I sank in my seat, hiding my face.

Maureen watched the woman in heels dart away in her black sedan, leaving only the loud slam of the front door behind her.

"Who was that?" Maureen spun to me once she was gone.

"It's Paul's ex. Or, I actually don't know what she is to him, but, either way, she's trouble." I scrambled through my words. "Patricia. I wonder what the hell she wants."

Maureen pushed open her car door. "Only one way to find out."

I held the massive door for Maureen, and she followed me into the history building. We moved directly for Paul's office. My pace slowed as I envisioned his reaction to our updates. He'd probably be angry for leaving him out of our rebirth rituals but it just seemed right to do it as privately as possible. But now I second guessed it, preparing myself for his response.

Just as I was about to knock on the fogged glass of his door, it pulled open, causing us to jump.

Paul nearly walked right into us, as if he were about to go after someone. He stopped short and stared at us with wide eyes.

"Wow. Stellar timing." He blinked his surprise away. “I was just about to go to the cottage to see ye.” His shoulders dropped a mile as he exhaled and turned back into his office. "Come in. Close the door." His voice chopped in quick syllables.

"Paul, there's so much to tell you. Things are happening and..." I struggled with where to begin.

He stood and spoke over me. "Were you at the cottage this morning?" He inspected us, checking our condition.

His question threw me off course. "Um, actually, no. That's part of what I need to tell you."

"You can't go back there right now." He shot a glance at each of us. "They're scouring the place for you, Izzy. There's word you haven't drowned and might have escaped the institution. They've a lot ta hide, you know, and will go to any lengths to keep their sins concealed." The worry lines in his forehead deepened.

My muscles liquefied. The thought of the nuns from the island coming after me was worse than any nightmare the catacombs could conjure. I couldn't go back to that place. I'd lose my mind for sure. But somehow, their power, the power of the church, seemed to breech all other laws, particularly if they felt they needed to cover up what had been done to me.

"I can't go back there." My voice shook. Thoughts of Jayne continuing to suffer the pressure from Sister Francis was enough to make me puke.

Maureen stepped closer. "Over my dead body."

Paul moved from his desk over to the window and looked out. "Patricia was here."

My spine straightened. "I know. I watched her leave."

He turned back to me. "Murt must have tipped her off. She knows I'm on a quest to find Maeve again."

My air sucked in.

He'd said it out loud.

I knew this was his motivation but to hear it made it real. He was on a quest to find Maeve again.

He continued, "And now Patricia knows too much. She knows about you, Isobel, and your gift. Murt told her everything about you and our mission in hopes of derailing me. He knows something. Something big. Or he wouldn't be going to all this trouble." He checked his phone out of habit but it remained dark. "We need to work fast before Patricia makes the connection that it was you who disappeared from the island. Murt doesn't know that part, thank Christ. He's assumed all this time that you had been released. But word will travel fast about your escape and she never misses a beat. Once she knows it was you who escaped, she'll tell everyone what you're up to and they'll be all over us."

My heart jumped into my throat and choked me.

"What the hell does she care?" Maureen spat.

His eyes fell. "She's never forgiven me for my crusade to find Maeve. She's probably right when she calls me obsessed." He looked at his phone again as if to redirect his wounded feelings. "She blames Maeve for our break up and for her nervous condition."

"She doesn't know what she's getting involved in," I interjected.

"Oh, she does," he retorted. "All too well."

I knew what he was talking about. I'd heard stories that she lost her mind back before Maeve disappeared. The local gossip said she had a nervous breakdown, but she had been affected somehow by the visions. Declan told me she'd been haunted or even possessed by an evil warrior and never recovered from the experience.

"I'm booked with meetings and classes through four." Paul squeezed his phone in frustration. "Can you stay hidden until then?"

My heart beat faster in my chest. Getting caught at this point would be catastrophic to our mission and the number of obstacles was growing by the minute.

"Meet us in Ballycroy. It's the only place for us to be right now," I said, planning our next steps.

He grabbed his leather bag and a few folders off his desk. "What do I need to know until then?"

"I think you've got the gist," I started. "Murt is an enemy, trying to steal the secrets of the tomb. He's turned Ryan against us. And Rory is back in the game."

"What?" Paul's voice boomed off the walls. "What the fuck is Rory doing in this?"

~

Hiding in plain sight was what Ballycroy felt like. It was the blazing hot spot of everything paranormal in my life, culminating in one intense location.

With only a couple days left until the solstice, my quaking knees proved it was too much time, too many people involved, and danger grew exponentially with every shaking breath.

I waited in the car as Maureen secured our rooms at a B&B a few miles out from the clearing. Shadows grew long across the hedgerows as early evening approached.

"Should be fine here," Maureen said as she climbed back into the car. "Owner's a widow, looking for company and a bit o' help with her mortgage. I told her we were visitin' friends and might be in and out at odd hours." She grinned.

I was glad to have an inconspicuous place to stay but it still wasn't enough to ease my anxiety.

"I have a strange nagging feeling." I rubbed the knots in my stomach. "I need to get back to the clearing. To Ryan. I need to be there for him."

Visions of his face flashed through my mind. His agony. And I couldn't bear it.

I'd seen his soul many times when we touched. It was pure. His intentions were good and I wasn't going to let go of that. I needed to fight for him.

Tears misted my eyes. He wasn't lost to me. There was still a chance to pull him back. To help him break free of whatever held onto him.

"Quick," I added, suddenly feeling like every second mattered for his safety. "I need to get there, Maureen. Now." I looked at the keys in her hand. "Do you mind if I drive?"

I pushed her little car into gear and pulled its best performance out of its peppy engine. My eyes remained fixed on the road ahead as we flew through the narrow carriageways along the Atlantic coast. Getting to the clearing and helping Ryan was my pure focus and I wasn't going to let anything stop me.

The crest of Doona Castle rose into view as I flew by the ancient cemetery. Then, slamming the brakes and leaving skid marks in the gravel, I stopped the car by Colm, who had escorted me down from the clearing after Ryan's assault. Rory's other clansmen gathered with him by the old church ruins.

Maureen braced herself on the dash and turned to me with raised eyebrows. "That's some driving, woman." She huffed. "Go on. Get up there." She nodded up the green hills.

I left her with Rory's clansmen and raced up to the clearing. Panting and pushing my fatigued muscles the final distance, I stopped at the boulders and rested my hands on my knees.

"He's been down there a good while now." Rory's voice practically shattered my fragile brain, causing me to jump. "His incessant screams are wearin' on me nerves." He chuckled.

I stood up and moved past the boulders into the clearing where Rory stood. In the same instant, Ryan's screams pierced my soul. The harrowing sound of his pain and suffering burst from the dark passageway like arrows through my heart. The echoes of his anguish tore at me, leaving me no choice.

"I'm going to him." I pushed past Rory and moved to the crevice that hid the entry to the tomb.

"Isobel, no. It's a journey he must make on his own." Rory jumped in front of me, forcing me to look at him. "You must allow him to fight his demons, his way."

"He's done that once already," I shouted as my panic rose with each of his blinding screams. "This is different now. The rules have changed." I sidestepped Rory. "I'm going down to him."

I wedged myself between the boulders and dropped my feet into the mouth of the dark hole. It had to be at least eight more hours until dawn, but Ryan's terrifying cries blew out through the cavernous depths, surrounding me with determination.

Rory reached for me, then stopped. His face grimaced in inner turmoil as he resisted the urge to block me.

"Keep Maureen safe," I said. "We'll be out at dawn."

The shake in my voice betrayed me and I shimmied into the cold, damp hole as Ryan's desperate wails shot terror into my soul.

CHAPTER 16

In a swift, fluid motion through the dark passageway, I found myself at the feet of the guardians, crouching as I searched for a safe place to hide. Ryan's shattering cries pierced my skull and I shook with fear, unable to imagine what could be tormenting him to that grueling level.

If I crept along the side of the tunnel, maybe I could enter the chamber without him knowing. That would give me a chance to figure out what the hell was going on and if anything could be done to help.

With one last stroke of the Keeper's stony feet, I pulled all my courage to my legs and forced them to move. Pressing my back against the side of the tunnel, I strained to see into the pitch darkness ahead of me. Following Ryan's blood-curdling screeches made it easy to go in the right direction and my innate knowledge of every detail of this journey kept me moving with confidence.

Reaching the end of the tunnel, I peered into the darkness of the chamber and in a flash, the altar lit up with flickering orange and red bursts. My eyes trailed along the catacombs toward the source of the glow.

Could it be the Immortal Druid? Had he come to help us?

My hope shattered into shards of pure panic as I stared at Ryan's writhing body engulfed in flames. His back arched against the stone floor and his clenched jaw bared every tooth in a brace against the agonizing pain.

In a sudden twitch, he flipped to his side, panting, as the flames faded. He gasped for breaths as if each could be his last and he was right—within seconds the flames grew and coursed along his body again, forcing a shriek of agony from his exhausted soul.

"Ryan!" I screamed, and jumped to him.

I tore my jacket off and flapped it over his body to extinguish the flames. My efforts made little effect as the licks of fire moved right through the fabric and onto my hands. I jumped back from the burning flames and watched them move up my arms and then away, with no pain, no heat.

Ryan's back arched again as he hit a level of pain that could break rocks in his tight jaw. My heart tore out of me at the sight of him suffering and I leapt to him again.

"Stop!" My voice split my ear drums with its force. "Show yourself, coward!"

Whatever or whoever was doing this to Ryan had to be stopped before they killed him.

I stared into the source of the flames each time they grew on him and there in a blazing funnel, like a gateway into Ryan's vision, I saw a giant man. He stretched taller than my eyes could see. Made of twigs and planks of wood, he lumbered closer through my mind and tauntingly shook his leg at me, exposing other tormented souls, writhing and burning within his engulfed structure.

The Wicker Man. From Ryan's nightmares.

Legend told that the Wicker Man predicted the future through human sacrifice and was the Druid's best means of time travel. But something wasn't right. The Druids were a peaceful society that obtained their great power through knowledge, enlightenment, and trusting the balance of nature. It had to be the rogue group who resorted to violence and human sacrifice as a quick means to their goals.

The Secret Society.

It was them.

They still had their claws in Ryan and planned to torture him to submission—to get him to be one of their pawns. Like Murt.

But Ryan was resisting. Like a warrior.

"Ryan! Keep fighting!" I shrieked. "I'll stop him!"

Flames grew higher along Ryan's anguished body and he jolted in muscle-locked pain while the Wicker Man laughed through the torture.

I stood over Ryan as the flames lapped around me and I reached through them to get to the bellowing man of wood. His broad shoulders exuded power beyond any mortal and his wild hair of crooked twigs and twisted branches fueled his intimidation. Each step I took only pushed him farther from my reach and I crumbled back toward Ryan's twitching body.

The echoing laugh of the Wicker Man lifted the hairs on my neck and he reached for Ryan, causing the flames to grow again. I couldn't bear another second of the torture and I dove on Ryan, wrapping my arms around him to dampen the fire.

Ryan gasped a breath of air as if I'd just revived him from certain death and he wrapped his arms around me in a hold that would never be broken.

"Isobel. No!" he cried into my ear. "You have to get out of here!"

His mind filled mine with his suffering and his endless fight. A fight to stay true to who he was. A fight to return to me.

I held him tighter, keeping the flames from burning him.

"I won't leave you. We can do this together. Hang on!" I yanked him to standing, never letting go, and my mind locked with his.

My bones grew stronger as his soul bonded with mine and his weakened form stood taller next to me. We stepped toward the funnel of flames that led to the Wicker Man.

I trailed my hand along Ryan's arm and interlaced my fingers with his. I squeezed his hand, and my mind brightened with more of his thoughts as he planned his attack on his torturer.

Together we charged and the flames grew higher. Our determination kept us moving in the face of danger and the Wicker Man slowed. He grimaced as his own flames torched hotter, fueled by our defiance.

He was soon engulfed in smoke and fire that twisted his vengeful face into the pain and suffering he had inflicted on so many others. The compounding fury and agony burst him into a fireball of destruction that blinded us with its intense heat and glare.

We clamped onto each other, blinking into the fading light as a storm of ash and soot whirled around us and blew into oblivion.

Then, there was only darkness.

~

Ryan reached for my face and moved his fingers over every part of it. His desperate apologies moved through my skin and tingled all over me. The tips of his fingers lingered on my lips and his insecurity caused him to hesitate.

His heart was true.

His intentions just.

My clear vision into his soul was unquestionable. He'd defeated his demon.

He was back and I wanted him.

My desire traveled through his fingertips and within a second his breath was on my lips.

"Isobel," he whispered. "You came back for me."

And his lips found mine. Cracked and rough from his torment, the feel of his anguished mouth sent my mind spiraling. I kissed him back, softening his lips with mine, and our minds whirled together in ecstasy.

We crumbled down to the floor in each other's arms and rested in a heap. Our hands explored in the darkness, moving along every body part but only with frustration. Our pure connection grew dull along the barrier of our clothing, only heightening when we touched the skin of each other's hands or faces.

Ryan released me in an instant and pulled off his jacket. Then his shirt. His fumbling in the dark made me smile and I pulled my own shirt off. I jumped to my feet and removed my shoes and pants as Ryan did the same.

Standing blind in the pitch dark, I hesitated, then slipped out of my bra and underwear. The sound of Ryan removing his own final layer sent chills through my entire body and I quaked with excitement.

We stepped closer.

Then reached for each other.

As soon as our bodies connected, a surge of light surrounded us and I stared into his eyes. The love I sent into him mixed with the same intensity that he shot back at me and we held on with a promise of never letting go.

"You're blowing my mind," Ryan whispered. "Quite literally."

"It's like you're woven into my mind. Into me," I said, closing my eyes to feel him more.

The glow around us became brighter as a beam of light entered the chamber from above.

Dawn.

It had finally come.

Time had passed by in an unmeasurable way. With nothing to see or do around us, time held its own measure and used it as it pleased.

We grabbed our clothing from the floor and exited the chamber in our purest forms, looking back at the magical hue that danced along the catacombs in the dawn's sacred light.

Leaving the hallowed space naked felt natural and right. We were our truest selves and had connected so simply and authentically in that state. It hadn't been a sexual thing. It was spiritual.

Darkness returned as we moved through the tunnel back toward the Keepers. Ryan went up the narrow passage first as I trailed my hands over the feet of the two guardians.

I was a new form of myself. Comfortable in my nakedness. All masks removed. Connected so intimately to Ryan. And I was a stronger form of myself with his mind entwined with my own.

As Ryan pulled himself out of the hole, I wriggled up the passageway and squeezed myself toward the opening. The brightness of morning shone on the portal to the world above and then Rory's voice blasted me into the reality of the day. My nakedness suddenly took on new meaning.

"Jazus, Ryan. Would ya put somethin' on ya? There's decent people about." Rory laughed.

"Turn yer head, Rory," Ryan snapped. "Isobel's on her way out. And she's in the same...condition." He hesitated a moment. "And keep yer mind out of the gutter."

Ryan's hand reached for me and I gripped it, knowing he understood what we'd experienced in the same way I did.

It was our truth.

I dragged my legs out of the hole and hunkered by the closest boulder, breathing hard. Exhaustion waved through me as the weight of gravity took its hold. I stared into the center of the clearing as my mind settled around itself.

Reaching for Ryan's hand, I caught his fingers with mine and allowed the rush of him to enter me again. And I smiled.

"Come now." Rory's voice broke my meditation. "Maureen'll have a conniption if she sees ya like this. Let's go." He shook his finger toward our pile of clothing and avoiding looking directly at me, encouraged us to join the world of the normal.

I reached for my clothes and with slow reluctance, I pulled them on, piece by piece. The more layers that went on, the more I craved to be naked again with Ryan. Next time, in our own space with our own rules.

Ryan smiled at me like he knew exactly what I was thinking. And he was thinking the same thing, only his thoughts involved more details of our bodies entwined and sweating.

My eyes grew wide with the shock of knowing what he was thinking. We could see each other's thoughts when we weren't touching.

"Oh my god!" I jumped and turned away.

"What the fuck!" Ryan blasted.

Once we broke eye contact, our thoughts cleared and became our own again.

CHAPTER 17

The idea of mind reading with Ryan, without having to touch each other, blew my mind. It changed everything. Our communication was in sync with even a glance and it felt like it increased our power together, exponentially.

But with two days until the solstice, I felt more unprepared than ever. Hiding away at the B&B would have been pure torture if it hadn't been for the distraction of researching and studying every detail of Druidry.

And every detail of Ryan.

If only Maureen hadn't been so old-school, we might have had more opportunity to explore. But our PG-13 time together was mind blowing on its own, and I tingled from the levels of intimacy we had enjoyed in such a short time. It was like all our layers of protection were gone, leaving us vulnerable to each other.

"What are you thinking?" Ryan's voice redirected my thoughts.

"Like you need to ask," I joked and avoided his eyes to tease him.

"I guess I'm still getting used to this whole thing. But, honestly, I could *always* read your thoughts. Your eyes always gave them away." He huffed. "I guess that's the case with most people, but no one slows down to take the time to see it."

He was so right.

And it relaxed me to know that we had always had the ability to read each other. Maybe not as clearly, but still, we always knew what the other was feeling. Just from the look in the eyes. It was easy, really.

And it explained why Murt avoided eye contact most of the time. He was hiding his true nature and his betrayal.

I thought about Paul. He always looked me directly in the eyes. It was why I trusted him.

And Maureen too.

And Gram. And Declan. And Michelle.

I thought more about the people I truly cared about. Those I knew.

Jayne. I knew her every thought from her eyes. And she wanted to get off that island. She wanted her life back. She would do anything for it.

I couldn't jeopardize the plans we had for the solstice though. But as soon as we were done with our mission, I would save Jayne. I wouldn't be able to function until I did. I missed her crazy-harlot-shit desperately.

"Well, I like knowing that you like me." I smiled.

"And that you are all I think about?" he jested. "It's a little embarrassing, having you know that." He looked down at my black laptop screen.

"I like that." I pressed the power button on the keyboard but nothing happened. I was desperate to learn more about the Druids and craved the internet and its wealth of links.

Ryan jiggled the plug and checked its connection at the wall.

"It's dead," he said.

"Yup. All technology. It's just going." I continued to press random keys, knowing something sinister was happening. Time was turning back, slowly.

I grabbed my backpack full of history books from Paul's office and pulled out one on medieval Ireland. I flipped through to the history of Grace O'Malley, chieftain to the O'Maille clan of the 1500s. Maeve was her descendent and had travelled back to her time. That was where all of this mess started.

Well, I imagined the mess started long before that, but the rift in time began back then. It must have been what led Maeve back there.

Ryan watched my page flipping. "So, basically, we go down the hole again tomorrow night. That will put us in position for the dawn of the solstice."

"Yeah. I know. It's almost here." I shuddered. "When Paul gets here in the morning, I bet he'll have us do all kinds of preparation all day in the clearing. He's thorough."

"To say the least," Ryan added.

"I just hope Rory has enough reinforcements to keep Murt at bay," I said. "There's no way Murt will miss this if he has any say in the matter."

I remembered the look in his eye when the dawn light illuminated a specific door in the catacombs. It was as if a treasure chest had been revealed to him. It made me nervous.

"Seems like Rory's got it covered. I mean, he's had clansmen there around the clock guarding the site. Murt wouldn't have a chance if he showed his face there." Ryan pressed his finger on a page, pointing to charts and pictures. "Look at that."

We followed a string of stories about Grace O'Malley's fleet of over two hundred men, her piracy, and her meeting with Queen Elizabeth I. But it was the more obscure data that pulled us in. The bits about Druidry and those with higher knowledge, beyond the science that was understood at the time.

These details were somehow connected to the stories of Grace O'Malley, before and after her lifetime. Though the legends after her were the ones that intrigued us most. Because these were the missing links that connected the past to Maeve.

"It says the Virgin Queen and the Sea Queen passed on the same day, in 1603," Ryan read aloud.

"Queen Elizabeth and Grace O'Malley. That's just weird." I looked up at him. "They had only met once, but knew each other to be kindred spirits. Two powerful women who reigned over their countries and did whatever they could to protect their people."

"And that's what the Druids have done for thousands of years too,"

Ryan added. “But it was around that time that the world started changing so fast. Growing and developing without parameters." The pages of the book nearly turned themselves as we leafed through the stories.

The door to the sitting room pushed open, causing me to jolt. My nerves lingered in flight mode perpetually.

Maureen peeked in.

"Tea?" She carried a tray of mugs in and placed it on the table by the modern tile fireplace.

I closed the book and moved it aside. She brought the cups of tea over and sat each one down in front of us.

"I need to share something with you both." She reached in her sweater pocket and pulled out a folded paper. She opened it and smoothed it out on the table with her palms. "It was written from memory. From a text message, just before the mobile phones went dead."

"Let me see that." Ryan reached for the paper and looked at the scrawled words. "What the hell?" He passed it to me.

I glanced at the sheet and read the reproduced lines of text conversation.

No worries they have no idea

Whats the plan for getting me in there then

Wear your cloak stick with me they won't suspect a thing if u stay close

And

And I send u down at just the right moment

"Who gave this to you?" I asked, staring at the signed name at the bottom of the paper.

Just as I began to decipher the Irish spelling of his name, Ruadri, Maureen answered, "Rory."

~

This complicated matters. Murt had found a way, an accomplice, to enter the tomb on the solstice and it was obvious who the weak link was that would allow him entry.

"How did Rory get this message?" I asked Maureen.

"He won't disclose his source," she said. "But he gave it to us as a warning. Said he knew he could never trust that guy."

"Paul." Ryan said out loud what we were all thinking.

My stomach dropped.

If Paul was planning to help Murt find a way into the tomb during the solstice, it would ruin everything. A sour taste climbed into my throat and filled my mouth. Paul would betray us. I couldn't believe it.

"But why would Paul want Murt to…" My voice trailed off as I answered my own questions.

Paul had one focus only. Finding Maeve.

He knew I had a broader focus. I had been chosen to close the rift in time, to reconnect the past with the future. I was the truth seer—the one entrusted with the knowledge and ability to disrupt the curse. It was vital that I succeeded, to ensure our very existence.

The ancient Druid's curse had already weakened our gifts and it was only getting worse. My visions had actually stopped all together. My last vision was of Rockfleet after leaving the island. The only thing that remained now was my ability to see into Ryan's thoughts and that was a result of our rebirth. And even Maureen struggled with accessing her second sight.

Everyone around us felt the devastation of glitching technology, ruing the tech companies, and some eccentrics began preaching of the approaching apocalypse. But the level of panic hadn't grown to jail-house riots, emptied grocery stores, and looting in the streets. The only explanation to the relative calm was that it was a natural progression of the curse. For the most part, it went unnoticed.

But we knew the truth.

Time was turning back on itself, just as the rogue society of Druids intended. It was their twisted way of preserving the mystical Celtic ways of the past.

But my focus also had to be on the modern-day witch hunt that stalked my every free, breathing moment. It distracted me from my focus on the solstice.

My eyes widened.

Was there a connection? Between the curse and my stalkers? It wasn't the first time I'd wondered this. I always felt that if I could end the curse, it would help stop the witch hunt. Somewhere deep within me I knew they were intertwined.

I stared at the cups of tea Maureen had placed in front of us, considering the possibility that Sister Margaret and her posse might somehow be threatened by me, and the other seers, because they knew we had the power to influence the future. And the past. They seemed to know the power we held better than we even did.

But no longer.

It was our time to take back the control.

It all began to piece together in front of my eyes, but scared the hell out of me even more. If my present day stalkers were connected to the curse, it could mean they were a part of the Secret Society too, somehow. The idea sent panic through my veins and I shook off the grandiose notion. But it wouldn't shake.

Then I thought about Paul's betrayal again and my fists clenched.

Finding Maeve was a pivotal part of this journey, he was right, but held no guarantees. I had to move forward in my mission of following the ancient ritual of the Druids, either way, and I was sure Paul had no intention of risking losing this opportunity. He needed Murt to help see it through and I hadn't realized it until now.

"Shit. They're going to sabotage it." Panic rose in my voice. "They'll go to the wrong area in the catacomb in search of her and will disrupt the natural course of the solstice illumination. Paul will be rushing, distracted by his obsession, and will make mistakes. We'll miss it then. They're going to ruin our chance."

I stood and pushed myself away from the table in exasperation. Ryan stared at the transcribed text message, as if hoping it meant something else.

I turned to Maureen for answers.

"They won't ruin our chance," she said with a smirk. "Not if we beat them at their own game first."

My mind raced all night, planning not only how we would face the solstice, but also how we would prevent Paul and Murt from disrupting the entire effort—disrupting my attempt at protecting our very existence.

Beating them at their own game was the way to go, like Maureen suggested. But how?

I had to trust the process. I had to have faith that the Druids would have predicted this. They would have known that others would want this knowledge. This power.

Keeping my heart open was proving to be the toughest part. It was so used to blocking itself for emotional protection, but now I had to believe in something I couldn't see or touch.

But I could feel it.

All around me.

Something was aligning and I'd never noticed it before. Something about the solstice. The rhythms of nature. It was all aligning and a pure sense of balance set me into motion.

Stuffing the final supplies into my pack, I topped it up and swung it onto my back like armor. With a deep breath, I left my room to find Ryan and Maureen.

Ryan's folded cot leaned on the wall just outside of Maureen's room, and her open door exposed an empty space. Sounds of plates clanging rang up from the kitchen and I followed the decadent smell of coffee.

"You couldn't sleep either?" I greeted them as they buttered their toast.

"Not much," Ryan replied, lifting his eyes to mine.

He was afraid. His fear poured out of him and chilled my core. Visions of me disappearing into the abyss haunted his mind and he couldn't control it. The Wicker Man pursued his every thought, leaving him unable to think or plan. He was frozen.

"I'm sorry." His eyes closed and he turned away.

I couldn't be surprised. It was no secret that Ryan struggled with all of this. From the very start he'd resisted his own gift and now, with me, he had everything to lose.

"I know we're walking into a lot of unknowns," I started. "But I need you with me. Okay?" I knew he would do anything for me but prayed he would be able to do whatever was necessary.

Maureen stood and brought her plate to the sink. "No better time than the present." She joined her new friend, Nora the B&B owner, to settle up for our stay.

Ryan passed me a thick piece of brown bread covered in butter and orange marmalade.

"If anything goes wrong, I'm fucked." He sat across from me and watched me devour my breakfast. "I'll do whatever it takes to get you out of there safely when this is done."

I swallowed a hunk of dry bread that made my eyes water. The thought of getting out of there safely seemed like a long stretch. But aside from any fears I had of what might happen in the tomb, I was relieved to not have to go into the hole alone.

I looked at the clock on Nora's wall. It was stuck at 3:12 and the second hand was still, but I knew it was probably around 7:00am, judging by the early morning light.

It was time to go to the clearing. Paul would be arriving shortly.

A shiver ran up my spine. Facing Paul, now that I knew his

misguided intentions, was going to be one of the most difficult things ever. I'd put so much faith in him. For years.

I'd have to play it just right, to the micro-t. I needed his support, even now. So as long as I had access to him, I would utilize his skills. Then at the last moment, I could shut him down, and shut him out.

My confidence in making contact with Maeve was strong and I was sure Paul would benefit as well, so stopping his attempts to usurp the mission would actually be helping him in the end. He wouldn't know that until later, though.

"It's time," I said to Ryan and Maureen. "Let's do this."

Before long, we were on our way to Doona Castle. Maureen followed us and kept close behind Ryan's truck.

"So what's the plan for halting Paul and Murt in their tracks?" Ryan asked.

I picked at my cuticles. "Act natural. Keep an eye out for Murt among the robed ones." I stared out my window as we approached the old church ruin. "And I'll talk to Rory straight away."

Numerous cloaked men milled around a few cars shoddily parked by the ruin. Rory's clansmen.

I studied their faces but they all became a blur of unfamiliarity. Paul's car popped out at me through the sea of brown robes but he himself was nowhere to be seen.

"Paul's probably already up at the clearing. Rory too." I unbuckled and opened my door before the truck was fully stopped. "Meet me up there?" I pulled my backpack after me as the tires skidded in the dirt.

"Wait...but," Ryan stuttered, then looked back at Maureen searching for a place to park. "Okay. I'll be up once she's settled."

"'Kay," I shouted back to him as my legs tore up the green slopes toward the clearing.

My heart raced out of my chest with sheer adrenaline. Muscular fatigue made no mention of its presence as I sailed up the incline.

This was it.

This was the moment I'd prepared for my entire life.

As the truth seer, I intended to believe whatever I saw and whatever I interpreted. I would listen to my intuition without question.

And right at that moment, my gut screamed.

I buckled over with a wave of nausea that could move mountains. Maybe it was my nerves. Maybe I was climbing too fast. But no. My gut spoke loud and clear, in no uncertain terms.

"Turn back," it ripped through me. "Run!"

CHAPTER 18

Uncertainty and consternation coursed through my veins as I realized I was going against my own intuition. The one thing I'd promised myself I would trust. But in this moment, I knew I had to move forward. Fighting the direct commands from my gut to run the other way, I pushed myself over the final ridge and entered the silence of the clearing.

I'd expected activity. Equipment. People. But the clearing was still and shrouded in a heavy blanket of mist that gave it an ethereal feel.

My eyes jumped to the boulders covering the entrance to the tomb. Movement at the top of one drew me closer and as the mist faded between us, I smiled at Rory. He sat at the top of the boulder with one leg propped on it as if he owned it.

"Mornin'," he called to me.

"Hi." I hadn't actually spoken with Rory in over six years and I'd forgotten how handsome he was. Even more so now. His black hair was always a little long at the top, falling into his eyes, but it was shorter now and tight around the sides, though still long enough at the front to flip up away from his face. "So, um, thanks for being here. It means a lot." My stupid words soured my own ears. I just didn't know where else to begin with him.

"Well, there's been no one down the hole since you and Ryan emerged," he stated. "I can assure you of that."

I blushed, remembering I'd been naked at that time, which made it even harder to talk to him now.

"That's a relief," I said. "I don't need any unexpected surprises down there. On top of whatever else is going to happen." I glanced around for Paul and his equipment. "Has Paul been up here yet? I saw his car below."

"No sign of 'im." Rory bit a nail and spat it out. "Not that I'm in any hurry ta see that guy. But ya can't always pick 'em, right?"

Shit. Rory and Paul were the two competing men in Maeve's life. Each had hoped to be with her. Paul had been winning, I think, when Maeve disappeared, but I was young and couldn't be positive on all the details.

They were both there the day she went into the mist. I would never forget their torment when they realized she was gone. Their hearts broke right there on the rocks, each in their own way, and their anguish had haunted me for years.

And now, they would both be here again, together. My eyes widened at the revelation. Things were lining up in ways I couldn't have planned or predicted.

"I saw the notes of the text message that you sent to Maureen," I blurted out. "Paul and Murt?"

Rory looked around to be sure we were still alone and moved to the edge of the boulder he sat on.

"Seems rather likely," he said. "Paul, I can work with. I know his motivation. But Murt, he's the problem. I can't tell what that fecker is planning."

An immediate sense of relief washed over me at Rory's comment about Paul. He seemed to have a similar grasp on his part in all of this. The Murt bit still worried me, but I was grateful to have Rory here with his clansmen if or when he showed up.

The memory of Rory's numerous clansmen below, by the church ruins, heightened my anxiety. Maybe Murt was lurking within them, waiting for his chance. I turned in the direction of the trail leading down to them and just as I blinked, Paul came into view.

"Isobel!" he called to me. "Grand. You're here." His smile lit up his whole face. He hoisted his huge duffel bag into the clearing and it landed with a clanking thud. "We've a good bit of time to get things set up and to devise a very specific approach."

His focus seemed to remain on our original mission, but I had to remember his true intention. And that it was somehow connected to the Secret Society and Murt.

I looked back through the clearing to Rory's boulder but he was gone.

"I've been researching the rituals around this event, like fire and drums," I said, acting as natural as possible. "It would be cool if we could recreate that somehow." I glanced around again for Rory.

"Absolutely. We need everything as authentic as we can make it. We can coordinate with Rory's clansmen. They're already gathering..." His words were drowned out by a louder voice.

"We've got it covered," Rory interjected with offense in his tone as he walked in from behind the boulders.

Paul flinched and stood taller.

"Hey, man." He reached his hand out to Rory.

Rory looked at it, then at Paul, and shook his hand.

"Don't fuck this up for us, man." Rory spoke into Paul's eyes without blinking. "It's a delicate process."

"Our agendas aren't that different, I'm assuming." Paul studied Rory's face. "Why else would you be here?"

Rory squared his shoulders and stepped into Paul's personal space. "I'm not completely sure of your agenda, McGratt. Never have been." His tone held more than threat. It held accusation.

"Back up, Rory," Paul spoke through clenched teeth. "There's work to be done here. Don't let that ego of yers distract from our purpose."

Rory stepped in even closer and lifted his finger, pointing it at Paul's chest. "You *let* it happen," he seethed.

And with that, Paul lost his composure and smacked Rory's hand away from his chest. He stepped right up to Rory's face with daggers in his eyes and I was sure their noses would touch.

I jumped at them and pushed them apart, throwing myself between them.

"Stop it. This is a waste of our time!" I shouted like they were children. "I need you to stay focused. You are both necessary here. Please."

I couldn't believe Rory had said that, basically blaming Paul for Maeve's disappearance. Damn.

Yet somehow, I knew each of them was critical to the mission. They had both known and loved Maeve. They were there when she disappeared. If I was to make contact with Maeve and try to reconnect her to our time, I would need both of them here for her.

A rustling of robes and voices approached the clearing and the three of us jolted to attention. Four robed clansmen moved into the grassy space and walked straight to Rory.

"We're set up below. Watchmen at every point," a loud voice boomed from the group. I recognized Colm in an instant and smiled. It was like he was Rory's right hand man, ready to assist at any moment. "Ryan's on his way up," he said to me with a nod.

"And Maureen?" Rory asked.

"She'll stay below with the others, keepin' watch at that level," Colm replied. "The rest of us will cover the perimeter here. No one will get through. I can assure you."

I remembered Colm's desire to be included in the skirmish that ensued when Ryan and Murt attacked me. His loyalty to Rory, following his request to escort me down to safety, was also unyielding. I smiled at his eagerness to be a part of the action again.

"Sound." Rory nodded and directed the other robed men to their points.

I studied each face and recognized none of them, but Rory seemed to know each one and assured me that Murt hadn't infiltrated the group. My eyes moved to Paul as I watched him observing the clansmen. I wondered if he was looking for Murt as well.

"Isobel." Ryan moved into the clearing, breathing hard from the climb.

He took me aside to the edge of the boulders and looked at the others to be sure no one was listening.

"It's Maureen. She had a fleeting vision below, like static, but still enough for her to see." His eyes stared into mine as he became lost in my conflicted thoughts about Paul and my fears of going into the tomb. He squeezed his eyes shut, as if to focus on what he was trying to say.

"She saw a curse awakening," he continued. "Surrounding the clearing with streaks of light that flashed skeletal faces wincing in pain and wailing with suffering." He panted. "The curse of the solstice."

"What?" I pressed against the boulder behind me.

"Designed to stop intruders, she said. To keep the location secret. And sacred." He paused. "It's not safe, Isobel."

My gut grumbled and tightened.

It was true.

I'd felt it on my way up here. It had never felt that way before. Something had told me to turn back. To run.

And now it was too late.

The amount of brown robes accumulating around the perimeter of the clearing made my nerves twitch. The shadowed faces turned to a blur after the eighth or tenth. With numbers like that, it would be easy for Murt to slip in. I lifted my eyes to Ryan's and he leapt to Rory's side.

I watched Rory's head bob as he counted his clansmen and then nodded to Ryan in assurance that all were accounted for. Ryan's shoulders relaxed and he moved back to the center of the clearing where I was assembling the fire.

"I don't know how to feel about the Paul thing," I whispered to him. "I think, if we can keep Murt away, then we have a chance at having Paul help us." I paused. "Without Murt, we might be able to trust him. A little." My eyes squinted at my weak attempt to give Paul a waiver for conspiring with the enemy.

But I knew how much we needed him. His knowledge of ancient Celtic rituals and his ability to interpret the symbols and ancient language carved in the catacombs made him beyond valuable. It was also his part in the larger story, Maeve's story, that made his presence necessary.

I almost forgave him in a way for his obsession with Maeve and his determination to get her back, no matter who stood between them. He would do anything to find her and I understood that.

Ryan watched Paul from the corner of his eye.

"I don't intend to spare him," Ryan said. "If he shows any reason of suspicion, I won't hesitate but to grab him and read his every thought." He hesitated. "Might not be a bad idea to do it right now."

I raised my palm to him. "Hold on. He knows your gift. Let's not put him on the defensive until absolutely necessary."

"You give him too much credit." He set a long piece of dried bog turf onto the pile for the fire.

"The way I see it, he has until the last minute to do the right thing." I crossed my fingers, praying he would choose to not betray us.

I stepped back from the pyramid of sod slices that had been cut from the bogs of Connemara. They'd been used for centuries in rituals like this one. Their heavy swirls of smoke and earthy smell set a perfect tone for historical rites of passage.

Several of the cloaked clansmen entered the clearing, leaving only a few at specific watch points. They moved with precision, as if they'd rehearsed the next steps for decades, and each took their place around the fire pit.

As if in a trance, they rocked in synchronicity while a low chant filled the air around us. The chant started out as a hum and with each new breath, rose in volume and vibration. The hairs on the back of my neck stood as the sound carried me to a place bigger than where we were. A place that held room for all of us. Together. As one.

I closed my eyes and joined in with the chant. Unsteady and choppy, the hum of my voice struggled to find its comfort level, but after three or four attempts, the sound found its place within the other voices.

The sound of the universe rose above us and I continued to breathe and chant until I'd lost all measure of time. Within the meditation came a heightened awareness of my true essence. My purest purpose. And I focused on it. On her.

She looked like me, only stronger. She was confident and playful. Her eyes were clear and her shoulders square. Her hair blew back from her face and she gazed at the horizon with an open heart.

She was the one I would take with me into the tomb. To face the curse. To return balance to the Druids and all who believed in the mystical realms of our existence. She would protect me. Guide me.

I was her.

She was me.

I inhaled deeply, connecting to her, fusing to her, and when I opened my eyes, a new voice awakened within the chanting.

"We celebrate in high places, in the eye of the sun, as we welcome the solstice," a clansmen stated. "We invite the sun's strength to the earth and welcome its life giving power." The voice moved through the other voices in a similar cadence, yet stood out on its on. "Light of the shore, we honor you."

The rhythmic chants rose in volume and speed as excitement mounted for the coming of the solstice. My heart pounded with the beats of the unified voices and with a final vocal punch, the chanting stopped.

My eyes shot open from the shock of the silence and I gasped. Darkness fell around us as dusk prepared herself for nightfall.

Time had passed so quickly while I was...in a trance. I'd entered a higher level of concentration than I ever had in my life. A linear focus that left me steady in my soul and clear in my head.

Smoke from the fire swirled throughout the clearing, making it difficult to see. I squinted into the gray wisps, searching for Ryan. His silhouette appeared to me by the boulders over the crevice and I flew to him.

"Oh my god. I don't even remember the fire being lit." I approached with an apologetic tone.

He smirked and looked at Rory. "You were gone for a bit there. Like, whoosh." His hand burst open, splaying his fingers like fireworks.

Rory laughed from high up on his chosen boulder. "Not the first time I've seen a newbie get taken by the chanting of Druids. You good?" he asked me.

"Yeah. I mean, I'm better than good." I inhaled deeply. "I'm ready now."

"So, what's the plan? You and Ryan?" Rory asked.

I closed my eyes for a second and watched the structure of the plan settle like tight puzzle pieces in my mind. "Paul, too," I said. "He needs to be right here, ready for whatever might be necessary."

“Okay,” Rory nodded without judgment. "McGratt!" he shouted across the clearing. "Yer up."

I reached for Ryan's hands and held his eyes with mine. "You ready for this?"

"A hundred percent. No way yer goin' down there alone."

It was true. He was there for me without waver. He didn't like what was happening but he was committed to doing what he needed to do.

"Thank you." I smiled into his eyes just as Paul's voice blasted from behind us.

He ran across the clearing shouting, and jumped like a skittish rabbit.

"Something's not right!" he screamed and pushed past us to the opening in the boulders. Leaning his head down the hole he yelled at the top of his lungs. "Maeve! No!" He fell backward onto his back. "Help her! She's in agony!"

I jumped back from him and stared. He thrashed on the ground as if fighting an unseen enemy. His cries continued as he called for Maeve to be helped.

His voice pierced through my soul, proving the time was here.

Time to face the demons that had been tracking me my entire life.

~

I jumped to Paul's side and helped sit him up. "Paul, it's okay. I'm going down to help her. Stay calm. I'll..."

He screamed again, this time as if he were the one in agony. His teeth clamped together so hard I was sure they would crumble from the pressure and his fists balled tight until they turned white.

"They're killing her!" he shrieked as his entire body contorted and he ripped at his hair.

Rory leapt down from his boulder and waved for a few of his clansmen to hurry over.

"It's the curse. The curse of the solstice," Rory explained as he nodded for his clansmen to move Paul from the passageway and out of the clearing. "I've heard of this. It keeps away anyone who should not enter."

Paul's screams continued to mix with the heavy smoke in the clearing and I covered my ears with my hands to keep my panic from rising to a level that would start my legs running.

"It's eleven o'clock. Dusk," Rory stated. "Time to go." He caught the look of fear in my eye. "No worries, now. We'll take good care of him." He nudged his chin at me to get going.

I reached for Ryan's hand again and squeezed onto it like a lifeline. I stepped closer to the opening to the passageway with him and looked into his face.

As soon as we had eye contact, my mind filled with the horror of the Wicker Man. He was coming straight for me with fire in his eyes and flames rising from every part of him. His intent was clear. He would stop me in my tracks and blow my ashes to oblivion.

"Ryan!" I screamed.

He dropped my hand and reeled back in terror. "Isobel!" he yelled, as if he couldn't see me. "Run!" He swung his arms at the air, fighting against the attack of his worst nightmares. "He's almost on you!" he shouted, stumbling into the clearing in an invisible battle.

Rory's clansmen surrounded him as he flailed, calling out to me in pure panic. "I'm sorry, Isobel!" He fell to his knees as if he'd lost the battle. "I'm sorry," he cried.

Tears streamed from my eyes as I watched him crumble within the protective circle of the clansmen.

"It's the curse, Izzy." Rory soothed me. "They see their worst fears. You need to stay strong. Fight it."

Rory's men removed Ryan from the clearing as he struggled against his invisible attacker. His desperate shouts carried on the wind and out to sea.

And I stood silent. Alone.

Tears fell heavy now as I stared at the dark hole in horror. The depths of its shadows taunted me.

"I'm going alone," I stated.

The idea was the most terrifying concept I could ever conjure. But in the next breath, I knew it to be right.

Rory reached for my elbow and walked with me to the crevice. I bent down and wiggled into the narrow opening and dropped my feet into the hole.

"I'll be here. And I'll greet you at sunrise." He released my elbow and as he let go, the world imploded on me with its full gravitational force as I took on the heart of a warrior.

"I'm scared," I said to Rory.

"I know." He nodded.

And I pushed myself down into the dark, harrowing passageway.

CHAPTER 19

At the bottom of the tight passage, I squeezed around the corner toward the statues of the Keepers. The darkness tweaked my flight response and I paused to steady my breath. The thick black in front of me was like a wall at first, but I allowed my other senses to take over and soon, I could see everything around me—from memory and touch and smell.

It was the start of the solstice and my nerves twitched in preparation for what it might bring.

I reached ahead of me and moved my hand along the base of the first guardian in greeting and then stepped to the other one to formally request passage. My shoulders turned in response to the damp, musty smell that wafted from the tunnel and I followed it like a welcome invitation.

Every nerve tingled as I trailed my hand along the wall of the tunnel, preparing to enter the catacombs. My heavy breathing bounced off the walls and echoed into my ears, raising my awareness of my singular existence.

My feet bumped along the uneven rock floor and I envisioned the smooth ocean rocks that were painstakingly placed there, one by one, to create the foundation. The sound of a small stone pinging behind me turned my head and my breath stopped. My ears flinched in the direction of the sound and I waited for more.

Silence.

In a whoosh of pent up fear and used air, my breath released from me in a huge exhale. "It's okay," I thought to myself. I just need to be prepared for anything.

I moved into the catacomb and took a deep inhale of the stale air. As I crossed to the center, my hands reached out and stroked the surface of the altar without even feeling around for it first. They knew exactly where it was and how tall it stood. I'd memorized every feature of the tomb and saw each detail as if light shone upon it all.

My fingers trailed along the side of the altar and found the carvings that led all around it. I walked in a steady pace, circling the altar, as my fingers read the graphics like a movie reel. Each loop around the altar conjured more vivid details that overlapped and wove into complex concepts. Mathematical and linguistical. My mind snaked through vibrant wormholes in the universe as the secrets of the Druids were revealed to me, expanding my thoughts to near explosion.

Then, in an instant, light flashed, illuminating the entire catacombs. I shielded my eyes from the sudden brightness. Had I unlocked something? A portal or a wormhole?

"You're wasting your time." A sour voice stunned me and I jumped to the far wall.

Staring into the beam of light, I squinted with my hand at my eyes.

"Who's there?" I barked.

The light dropped a few inches off my face and I stared into Murt's evil eyes.

"Sorry to disappoint. It's just me," he said. "Here to take care of business long unfinished."

My knees turned to jelly.

"You're going to ruin everything." I shuddered from the shock of his presence and questioned my personal safety. "Please. Leave. You might have already ruined it."

I stepped toward him with an anger that started in my feet and moved through me like hot liquid metal, replacing any fear that dared to begin. Then I paused in my spot, wondering how he'd even gotten down here.

"How did you...how," I stuttered.

Somehow, he'd got past Rory. And somehow, he was unaffected by the curse that surrounded the clearing. It made no sense.

A smirk of arrogance rose up his face and he stepped toward me.

"You have no idea what you're dabbling in. You're green." He spat his words at me. "I'm a traveler, Isobel. Stuck in the misery of limbo. Sent long ago by my order of Druids, to stop you." He huffed. "To allow the turn back of time to become complete. And I intend to end my purgatory now and regain possession of my soul."

I stepped back from his advance as my heart pounded like a drum in my ears.

His intentions were of a selfish nature. To end his own suffering from being caught between two worlds, living lifetime after lifetime, waiting.

"Murt. Let me help you," I said in a steady tone, barely able to hide the shake in my voice. "If you let me complete this ritual, it might help you, too."

"And if it doesn't? Another year to wait for the next solstice? Another century for it to realign correctly?" he snapped at me. "I'm done waiting. Now is my time."

He pushed past me with a hard shove that sent me into the wall with a thud. A sharp pain stung my forehead and I reached for it, feeling a trickle of blood roll past my temple. I winced against the ache from the hit and blinked to clear my vision.

Turning back to Murt, I gasped as I watched him lurch to the catacomb doors and begin pulling on the one that had been illuminated during his last visit here.

"Stop!" I shouted and jumped toward him. "You don't know what you're doing!"

He turned to me like I'd slapped him and his face contorted with centuries of suffering and aggression. Like a steamroller, he barreled into me, grabbing hold of my shoulders, and pushed me across to the other side of the tomb again. He pinned me against the limestone wall and seethed his venomous words into my face.

"Stay back, bitch. You're nothing. A speck in the universe and I won't hesitate to stop you with greater force." He pushed my shoulders harder into the stone wall. "This is *my* time now." His foul breath in my face made me turn from him but he continued to force his strength on me in a final show of dominance.

He stepped back then and pulled an object from inside his coat. The glint of metal widened my eyes as I watched the length of the dagger emerge from his jacket.

Panic burned my ears as he traced the outside of my face with the point of the knife.

"Do we understand each other?" he asked.

My words caught in my throat and I nodded in agreement.

"Good," he said while taking steps back toward the catacomb hatch without breaking eye contact with me.

He turned then and in a swift motion, plunged his dagger into the edge of the small door, prying the seal open along the top and down one side.

Such a violation of the sanctity of this sacred space made my stomach turn. Adrenaline coursed through my veins as I watched him desecrate the restful tranquility of the crypt with his impatient, clumsy efforts.

I pushed off the wall as courage exploded within me. There was no way I was going to watch him mess everything up. Even if it meant facing a dagger in the hands of a crazed time traveler.

Long, powerful strides carried me to him and I grabbed on to the shoulders of his brown cloak. I yanked as hard as I could and twisted with a jarring spin.

Murt fell back and rolled from the force of my grab and dropped his knife in the process. The clang of metal on stone reverberated through the chamber and my ears ached from the pitch that pounded in them.

A strange rustling moved through the chamber, same as what I'd noticed my other time down here, and I tried to follow it.

Then Murt scrambled to his feet with rage flashing from his pupils and just as he prepared to launch at me, the door he'd been prying popped open with a creak. Dull orange light glowed from the narrow openings along the edges of the door and we stared at its mesmerizing haze.

In an instant, Murt flew to the door and pulled it fully open.

"Wait!" I shouted.

But he ignored my command and stared into the flickering light of the open chamber. His eyes widened as a smile spread across his face.

"This is it!" he squealed. "My salvation!"

He leaned in further as I pressed back against the wall, putting as much space between me and the open door as I could. I turned away, not wanting to set eyes on whatever had put that look of enrapture onto Murt's face.

As my eyes diverted, they fixed onto the shadow of the Immortal Druid. He faded back into the wall with his hands in a prayer position, nodding his head at me in a steady motion. His robe rustled along the wall as he blended into it.

My heart exploded in my chest as I silently thanked him for being the steadfast Keeper of the Ovates. He'd served them well.

Then Murt's squeals pulled my attention back to him. His elated tone turned to a sickening sound of torture and anguish that filled every space of the catacombs, sending terror through me.

Murt blasted back from the open door, screaming in pain as he swatted at flames engulfing his arms. He fell back onto the ground and rolled, smothering the flames that only rose higher with his efforts.

His screams grew louder and more piercing and he turned back to the open chamber in shock. As his eyes focused on the inside of the burial vault, he fell silent for a moment, and then his entire body began shuddering. He scrambled up to run but flames licked at him from the chamber and grabbed onto his ankles.

"No! You're mistaken!" he screamed. "I'm here to stop her! I will accomplish what was intended."

I glanced back, shielding my eyes with my hands as I watched the long, spindly fingers of the Wicker Man reach out of the vault. He pulled Murt across the stone floor, sending sparks and flames all over his body. Murt writhed in agony as he fought to escape the torturous grip.

Looking back to me, he reached for my hand, begging for me to save him. "Isobel! Help me!" he screeched.

Shit!

I had no choice. Every ounce of my being insisted on helping him.

I leapt to him, preparing to smother the flames with my body like I did for Ryan, and I caught the eyes of the Wicker Man. His mesmerizing gaze held mine and I danced with the flames in his deep pupils. The flares took the shape of people. Hundreds of people. The souls of those he consumed.

His massive wooden arm lifted with the weight of twenty men within it and he forced me back with a broad swing. Stumbling toward the far wall, I gathered my balance and turned back for a second attempt.

But it was too late.

He'd lifted Murt's thrashing body and dropped it within the cavity of his chest, piling him on top of other sacrificial sufferers. More flame burst around the Wicker Man as if fuel had been added to him and he spun into a vortex of smoke and fire, twisting into a narrow funnel that shot back into the vault.

The door slammed shut, removing all light and sound from the chamber and I was left, again, in pure darkness and isolation.

A faint scream far off in the distance broke the silence of my entombed isolation. I blinked into the thick black all around me and focused on the sound of the cry. It came from every direction in the catacombs and I fought to escape it but the more I resisted, the louder it grew until all at once, the sound came to a central point of explosion.

My mouth.

Screams tore out of me. One after another. Again and again.

I'd lost my mind. I was sure of it.

I grabbed my hair and pulled. Throwing myself back against the wall, I banged off it over and over, trying to smash myself back to control. My screams slowed then and I slid down the wall into a heap on the cold floor.

Parched and panting, I lay on my side in a fetal position. "Please God, let the dawn come. Please," I prayed while squeezing myself tighter.

I fought to understand what had happened to Murt. The chamber he'd been pulled into was too small to hold a man. And the door had closed tight with him inside.

Inside with the Wicker Man.

Lost to eternal suffering.

The legend was true.

And now I awakened to the truth in all legends.

With easy rocking motions, I soothed myself to a restful state. The wait would be far easier if I remained calm and patient.

I allowed my thoughts to roam and then to spiral in new directions. It was as if my mind's eye traveled without my body and observed everything in its path.

My vision trailed through wormholes in the time continuum and ejected at Rockfleet. Maeve's lifetime played out before me in fast forward and I watched her rise up to be a great leader of her people with a man she called Rí by her side. The two danced as entwined partners through their years. At the twilight of their union, they remained joined by the heart as one.

A lump welled in my throat and I struggled to swallow.

The final scene at Rockfleet showed the two lovers in their final moments. Rí passed away an old man in his sleep and that same night, Maeve faded into oblivion.

My eyes shot open and I stared into the black nothingness of the catacombs.

I blinked the images into my permanent memory and studied them in great detail. My thoughts moved away on their own again and traveled through the vortex of time, showing me the struggles of ancient Ireland and its painful disconnect from its mystical ways. A ripple in time, caused by the Druid's curse, had left imbalance in the land of legends.

However, one connection remained. It was strong enough to find its way through the abyss and my mind's eye landed on the time before Maeve disappeared. Somehow, she'd made the time leap and probably more than once. I had to believe she could do it again. With my help.

I hovered over her early years in Boston as she ran from her haunting visions and then her time in Ireland when she learned the truth of her curse. She was a descendant of the pirate queen, Grace O'Malley, and was destined to close the time gap between the 1500's and the present.

It was only after meeting Rory and Paul that she was able to piece it all together. Rory was a descendent of Rí and Paul a descendent of Grace's lover, Hugh. They were all responsible for pulling it together.

And Rory and Paul were here, above. Now.

A gentle hum started deep in my throat and I let it grow until it escaped from my mouth. Then came another hum until it formed into its own chant. The sound of my lulling voice filled the chamber, bringing life and tranquility into it.

As a new sense of calm washed over me, my eyes fluttered open in response to a gentle yellow glow. Had my prayers been answered? Dawn had arrived?

I pushed myself up to sitting, elated that I had survived but confused that I still held no answers.

I blinked into the direction of the glow and gasped at the vision of another brown cloak moving toward me. Just as my fight response prepared to hurtle me toward the aggressor, I locked eyes with the Immortal Druid.

Desmond.

I stood in my place and allowed his eyes to study mine.

"The truth seer returns for the dawn of the solstice," he stated.

"Yes," I replied.

"You have proven yourself worthy. There is no doubt you are the one." A gentle smile crossed his face. "You must take what time is left to complete your journey."

My breath caught short in my chest. "But I don't know what to do now."

"Oh, but you do." He nodded. "You are safe now, child. Use your gift. Use it well." His voice faded and the light grew dim.

"Wait!" I begged. "What will happen to you?"

"I will be released. And my gratitude to you will be infinite." He stepped back and blended into his space in the wall as the light disappeared with him.

Oh my god.

He was so sure of me but in reality I had no idea what to do. My head fell back in despair and after lifting it again, dizziness overwhelmed me. I stumbled forward and smacked my hands onto the altar.

The altar.

It held the magic. The mystery.

Instructions.

It was the portal.

I placed my fingers in the grooves of the carvings along the sides of the altar and walked around the perimeter, reading its secrets through my touch. I walked faster and the ideas became more complex. Faster still and the information took animated form and I dove into the powerful realm that opened up to me.

Bright light illuminated my mind as if preparing me for an epiphany that would rewire me. I waited, flexing my mind to keep it open to whatever might channel through. But instead of answers and true understanding, I felt chaos and blasting winds.

Howling gusts blew past me and light twisted in a whirling haze creating a dizzying assault to my senses. I pressed through the force of the winds and squinted for a glimpse of whatever might be around me.

Hair slapped my face in stinging lashes and tears tore out of my eyes, streaming along my cheeks. As I batted my hair down and planted my feet beneath me, I peered into the eye of the storm and zoomed in on a figure far out in the vortex.

I stared as it came closer, growing larger. The figure struggled in the blasts of wind and whirling chaos and bent with arms lifted protectively at the head.

Then she got closer.

A woman.

Her dress flowed in the gusts, creating ripples of fabric along the edges of the vortex. Chain mail hung from her shoulders all the way to her waist, leading down to the length of a sword that hung from her belt.

I stared in awe at her medieval majesty.

And then my heart skipped a beat as I recognized her.

"Maeve!" Her name blasted from my lips and I reached into the spiraling wind for her. "Maeve!"

She clawed through the swirling tempest and her face contorted with an agony that would have taken centuries to form. And then her mouth opened.

The sound that escaped her brittled my bones to dust. Its despair and suffering was more than I could handle and I screamed for her. I moaned and wailed for her pain in hopes of alleviating even a slight amount of it.

In a panic, I cried out to her again.

"Maeve! Come to me! Reach for me! Now!" My dry voice was hoarse and I begged it to rise up. "Reach bitch!" I cried out.

Her eyes met mine and everything around us buzzed in a vibrating stand-still. We hovered in a moment of purity that reconnected us to one another.

"Isobel?" Her voice shook and echoed in my mind.

"Reach for me, Maeve! Reach!" I begged her.

Her hand extended past her sword and beyond the gusting whirls of mist. She reached for me through oblivion.

"Oh my god, Maeve! Keep fucking reaching!" I commanded her. "Reach!"

Her eyes blinked into a focus that was new to her. She emerged into my realm like a newborn adjusting to the gravity, the climate, the light.

Her guard dropped then as she trusted me. She trusted me to pull her through.

And I reached for her.

I stretched into the unknown layers of the whirling vortex, wondering if I'd get pulled to the other side, never to be heard from again.

I shook my terror aside as I reached harder.

"Maeve! Grab on to me!" I shouted.

She stretched with all her might, her eyes popping with the effort.

Holy shit, I was about to touch her, and bam!

We connected.

Our energies merged and whirled within each other. My mind exploded with the content of her consciousness and I screamed from the overwhelming assault of information on my meager existence.

"Hold tight!" I shouted. "I'll pull you through!"

I yanked with all my strength, pulling on her wrist.

"Harder!" Maeve called from the beyond. "Pull, Isobel!"

I gripped her hand as if it was the one thing that could save her life. And save the life of Gaelic Ireland, and everything we lived and breathed. I squeezed her hand and I pulled with every ounce of power left in my body.

Bright light blinded me and I lost sight of her.

I blinked into the wall of white, trying to readjust my eyes.

I'd touched her. I knew I did.

Our fingers interlaced. Our palms sent heat and life into each other's souls.

I blinked into the light, searching for Maeve. For even a shadow of her.

And then I focused in on the light of dawn filling the catacomb.

CHAPTER 20

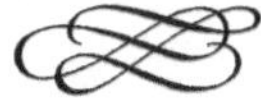

Dawn's early light illuminated the catacomb like a bolt of lightning. I panted against the wall, reaching for the shadow that was once Maeve.

She was gone.

The portal had closed.

I'd failed.

Dawn came before I'd had the strength to pull her to the other side. Our side. And now, I'd have to live with the knowledge that she was suffering in the abyss, pleading to be pulled back to a realm she knew. A realm she loved.

I sat and waited.

I waited for the Immortal Druid, who wouldn't come. He knew I'd let them down.

I waited for Maeve to materialize and blink into the light of her new day.

I waited for balance and rhythm to return to Gaelic Ireland.

My misery took me over. Could I live with being a failure?

I sat taller, defending myself against defeat. I'd come too far. I'd fought too long. This wasn't what was meant for me.

In my defiance, I followed the beam of light that dawn brought upon me. It glowed in a way my eyes had never seen before.

It pulled me. It led me.

I followed the light and my eyes trailed along the doors of the catacombs. The light moved across each alcove, leaving a hue of golden yellow upon the individual recesses, and it passed by the specific one Murt had violated. And was now entombed within.

The light continued to move and glowed brighter on a different door.

The vault lit up with a glow that left no question.

It was Maeve's tomb.

It was the location that she had been laid to rest with everything that mattered to her and right now, at this very moment, I was granted that knowledge.

I stepped closer to the vault.

Closer to Maeve.

I placed my hands on her grave.

My fingers tracked along a subtle carving on the door that only my sense of touch could see. I traced it and then gasped as the shape played out in my mind. It was the symbol Maeve had shown me in my first vision of her in this chamber—a Celtic knot of two hearts, one upside down, laced into each other.

With a crack, the seal around the door broke and light shone from within.

I jumped back and stared into the glow that emanated from the depths of her resting place.

Squeezing my eyes shut, I willed away the negativity, the possible curses that might surround the revelation of a burial place that was meant to be left undisturbed.

But my eyes pressed open against my better judgment, and I peered into the tomb of Maeve Grace O'Malley. Chieftain to the O'Maille Clan, circa 1600s.

I flinched as I reached into the unknown of the small chamber. I stretched my hand toward a lone box made of hand carved wood. I grabbed onto the box and pulled it out of its place of waiting.

I sat on the floor and positioned it in front of me.

Looking up toward the beam of the light of dawn, I drew a huge breath of air and focused on the box. With a momentary sense of courage, I untied the cracked cordage around it and propped the top of the vessel open.

I inhaled another full breath. One that would sustain me for longer than needed, if necessary, and peered in.

A single leather pouch. Tied with more of the same cordage. It sat in the ancient container, boasting its worth as if it were a crown of jewels.

I pulled the pouch out of its confines and balanced it on my knee. I untied the brittle leather cord, the bag wobbling amidst my prying.

I lifted the bottom of the sack and shook the contents out onto my palm.

As the object hit my hand, my adrenaline soared to a point that couldn't be contained and I shrieked.

"Oh my god! The ring!" I screamed at the top of my lungs and threw myself toward the tunnel.

I'd thought the ring had been lost forever. I'd left it behind in the late 1500's when I saw Maeve at Rockfleet.

"Ryan! Paul! Rory! Get me out of here!" I screeched as I ran through the dark tunnel toward the Keepers.

At the feet of the guardians, I stopped.

A sense of wonderment filled me and it was as if they wanted more information. They'd been watching for so long and now, finally, something was happening. Something they'd been waiting for over the centuries.

"I made contact with Maeve," I told them. "I have her ring! The ring of the pirate queen."

Their silence froze my muscles and I squeezed the pouch in my hand to be sure it was real. I reached into the pouch to pull out the ring of the pirate queen for them to see.

But instead of the ring emerging, a small scroll of parchment popped out first. One that wouldn't be ignored.

"Oh, wait," I murmured to the statues that had offered me safety and companionship throughout my subterranean quest. "There's more here."

I felt the scroll of parchment in my fingers, wondering if the Keepers knew it was there and wanted to be sure I didn't miss it.

"I need light," I said aloud. "Thank you. For everything." I pushed myself up the narrow passageway, close enough to the opening where morning light lingered.

I pulled the parchment from the pouch again and opened it with care.

It was a letter, written in black ink scrawl that resembled something Queen Elizabeth would have written.

Dearest Isobel,

Believe it.

Believe all of it and bring me back.

You are the truth seer and I depend on you to bring me home.

Rebirth, Isobel. Rebirth through the solstice.

Maibh

My air sucked in, choking me.

With a cough, I grabbed firm hold of the pouch with all its contents from past centuries and pushed myself into the light of day.

The dawn of the summer solstice greeted me as I emerged from the depths of the catacombs. Ryan grabbed my hand and pulled me up into his exhausted arms.

His embrace nourished me with vital life-giving energy but gnawed at me for information about what I'd encountered. At the same time, the torture that kept him from going down into the hole with me still quaked through his bones. But he was strong and his inquiring mind was pure. I trusted his need for the knowledge of my journey without question.

But no matter how long he held me, it would never be enough for him to completely understand the complex levels of my experience. It was a journey that could never be recreated with images or stories but had expanded my mind to a clarity that I hoped to be able to share with him over time.

Rory pulled me further from the hole as Ryan moved toward the center of the clearing. He stood back, allowing Rory to take over and he stared at me, knowing I'd reached a new level of enlightenment that even his gift couldn't fully comprehend. Ryan's eyes remained focused and eager for more though as it was clear that I allowed him full access into my thoughts. And he knew I wanted him there.

As I began to stare into the clearing to allow the events to settle fully into my being, my attention moved to the subtle rumble of a jet flying overhead. Then my focus pulled back to the hole and I watched Colm peering into it, as if waiting for something more to happen. He turned to me with his head tipped to the side with a look of confusion pinched between his brows.

My mind pieced together his thoughts in an instant. He was searching for Murt, waiting for him to emerge from the hole. His shoulders sank with each passing moment as he realized Murt wasn't coming out. There would be no celebration for them. No moment of glory. The bewilderment in his eyes outed him as I homed in on his deviant soul.

"He won't be coming out," I yelled to him. "Taken by his demons. He's gone."

My brazen tone pulled Rory's attention to us.

Colm's eyes grew wide in terror as he glanced back into the dark depths of the catacombs. A rush of stale air blew out from the hole engulfing him in the stench of death. His hood fell back from the gust, exposing his quivering lips and his loathsome cowardice. He scrambled back from the hole, smacking into the boulder behind him. Reaching for the back of his sore head, he stumbled outside of the border of the clearing and ran.

I nodded to Rory, confirming the betrayal of one of his trusted clansmen. Colm had foolishly revealed himself and Rory now understood the level of treason within his clan. He nodded back to me, acknowledging his discernment of the deception and then dropped his eyes in regret.

In the next moment, Rory had his clan rallied and they stood unified as they heard the news of Colm. Their instructions were easy to understand by the sight of their squaring shoulders and then by their structured organization into a unified manhunt.

Colm had been Rory's most trusted clansman. He'd snuck Murt past his guard, likely through distraction, exploiting Rory's faith in his loyalty and now, he had an entire clan after him.

A twang of guilt shot through my veins as I realized Paul hadn't been the defector after all. He was with us the entire time. It had been Murt and his minion Colm who held ill will against our mission. But they'd lost and Colm would soon be writhing in the painful knowledge of Murt's fate. And his own, as a traitor to his clan.

I looked back to Ryan waiting at the edge of the clearing, allowing me the time needed to process everything that had happened in the hole. Rory joined him, certain to not miss any new developments. But I'd already come to terms with my discovery and my experience. I understood the vital message without needing time to meditate on it.

I was the truth seer.

And my sight was clear.

Maeve's note asked for me to return her to her life in the present. To complete the circle. Rebirth.

I stared at her handwritten request and pushed my mind to its limits trying to decipher it.

Rebirth. Rebirth through the solstice, it read.

I gasped and stared into Rory's eyes. "She needs us. Still. It's unfinished!"

"McGratt!" Rory shouted.

I gazed into the center of the clearing, processing all I had encountered while waiting for Paul. His presence was paramount.

Rory, Paul, and me.

We were Maeve's team.

The ones to bring her back.

~

Paul stumbled into the clearing, ashen and exhausted from the abuse of the curse of the solstice, but as soon as he saw me he hurled himself to my side.

“Did you see her?” he begged.

I nodded but dropped my eyes. “Yes, but she is still trapped. She’s waiting for us to find her.”

"I knew the moment you emerged from the hole. 'Cause the terrors finally stopped,” he grumbled. “But their poison still runs in my veins, proving to me it is unfinished.”

He glanced around the clearing, likely still on guard for any sign of Murt. "Tell me. Tell me it all." He watched my every move, taking in every detail for analysis.

Ryan and Rory gathered around us and created a small circle of quiet discussion as I told them everything that had happened in the catacomb. I placed the ring in the grass in the center of our circle and all eyes gazed on it like it held the power of the universe.

And maybe it did.

"It's the one true connection to Maeve," Paul said, running his hands through his hair with a look of bewilderment splashed across his face. "What can we do with it?"

I reached for it and pushed it back into the pouch. "I don't know yet." I unrolled the parchment. "If I had had it when I made contact with her, when we touched, maybe I could have passed it to her." My head shook in disappointment at the mixed up order of events.

Rory leaned in further. "I don't know. She intentionally sent the ring back to you. To this time." He paused. "She wanted it here, now, for some reason."

"To close the continuum? To bring all events full circle. For closure," Paul speculated. "And the letter. There must be something in it we're not understanding."

"It's all about rebirth and seeing the truth," I murmured.

Seeing the truth.

I squeezed my eyes shut and thought hard. What was I missing?

The truth.

It was revealed to me and I still hadn't figured it out.

"We need Maureen," I blurted. "She's the Keeper of the Ovates. She's got to have some knowledge about this." I hopped up with no time to waste.

We flew down the trail leading back to the cars, leaving behind us several cloaked clansmen to continue their watch over the sacred grounds.

Morning sun washed across the sea, dancing and celebrating the start of its longest day. Shadows stretched behind Doona Castle as the front walls glistened in the golden rays.

Wet grass and squishing turf bounced beneath my feet as we hurried down the sloping green hills to find Maureen. The clear morning sky was a treat that might only last a short time before the typical mist and gray clouds rolled back in, and I delighted in the feeling of rebirth that the light filled me with.

Rebirth.

Everything was new.

Each new day.

We sailed toward the church ruins where Maureen stood, leaning against her car with a steaming tin mug of coffee in her hand. A small campfire smoldered along the side of the road and a clansmen poked the coals around a metal pot.

"A fine lookin' bunch ye are!" she hollered at us with a laugh. "Tell me now. What'd ye find?"

"So much, Maureen. Everything," I exclaimed, reaching into the pouch for the ring. "Yet, nothing." My tone took a dive, leaving no question for Maureen that Maeve was still lost in the abyss.

"Nothing?" she repeated.

She reached into her pocket and pulled out her mobile phone. With one press of its side button, the phone glowed to life and vibrated.

I gasped, immediately recalling the airplane that flew overhead as I emerged from the catacomb.

Was time was moving in the right direction again?

“Can it be true?” I stared at the others as they checked their own phones.

“My sight is clear now, Isobel. It’s been restored,” Maureen stated with a grin. “Well done, young lass.”

My breath huffed out of me. It worked. Partly, anyway.

Somehow, my contact with Maeve through the vortex had been enough to close the rift in time. It connected us for the briefest of moments, but it must have been enough.

"I made contact with Maeve,” I told Maureen. “We touched. I think our connection may have closed the gap. It might have been enough to end the curse." Speaking the words aloud confirmed the intensity of our contact.

Maybe what had occurred was everything that was meant to be.

"Yes," Maureen agreed. "I felt it. Balance was restored in everything around me." She nodded as if it was all coming clear to her. "I have a sense of peace deep within me now. I think you succeeded, Isobel Ross. You broke the curse."

Rory, Paul, and Ryan took a step back from me at exactly the same time and stared.

"Yes, gentlemen. I see you recognize her. The Truth Seer." Maureen finished the last sip of coffee in her mug. "Go on, now. I'm sure yeh've much to discuss still. Don't mind me. I'm well looked after by these gents." And she smiled a flirtatious grin. Then she turned to me with sharp focus in her eyes and whispered, “The truth seer never stops searching for the truth,” she said.

My eyes widened at her words. They were more than just a comment. They were a directive.

I turned toward the castle and filled my lungs with fresh morning air. As I exhaled, the air stuck in my throat and a thought exploded in my mind.

"The castle." A shudder ran through my body. "It's a part of this legend, too.”

It was the exact location where Maeve disappeared six years earlier. Rory and Paul knew it too.

We had to search it. It could hold the final clues to restoring her.

The truth.

My legs carried me toward the castle before another word could be spoken. And then my gut screamed to me.

"Run!" it commanded. "Run to it!"

With my eyes fixed on the high walls and jagged ramparts of Doona Castle, I ran across the grassy fields toward the ancient stronghold. Rory, Paul, and Ryan kept pace with me.

Doona had been a ruin when I first set eyes on it six years ago, but after Maeve disappeared, somehow, it stood proud in its full majesty as if never enduring the ravage of battles and the crush of time. I knew this place was mystical—connected somehow to the rift that had been created in time.

And now, now that the gap was closed, I wondered if there would be any new effect on the fortress.

The three men followed close behind me while Paul and Rory recalled their earlier experiences at the castle through huffed breaths. Each one shared a different perspective on the events surrounding Maeve's disappearance but their sense of loss held similar pain.

"It was the ghostly three that came for her. They took her into the mist." Paul spoke like it was still beyond his belief.

The ghostly three? I gasped as the memory flooded me. I'd blocked out the vision of the medieval clan people who came for Maeve that day. It was more than my young mind could handle at the time. But now, I remembered them and their faces. Particularly the face of the woman. Maggie.

My heart burst as I remembered my meeting with Maggie at Rockfleet. She was the one who took me to Maeve. Her essence wove deeply throughout this legend and I smiled thinking of her role in all of it.

Then Rory's voice pulled my attention back.

"I had her hand. She was going to take me with her." Rory's voice trailed into the breeze. "If only I hadn't lost her in the feckin' wind." He balled his fists as he stumbled along the rocks.

Their voices grew silent then as we approached Doona and slowed our pace. It was the last place Maeve had ever been seen in this present-day time and our somber silence reminded us all of the horror of that day. Grief laced the air as we each stepped around the stony walls in our own directions of contemplation.

Remembering Maeve.

Light mist coated my face and I turned to the sky. A blanket of gray crossed the horizon, filtering the sun to a gentle glow. The dull sky matched the heavy emotions that filled the air around us.

I walked toward the front of Doona and glimpsed Rory and Paul coming around from the other side. The three of us gathered together again and gazed across the rocks and out to sea.

I turned to find Ryan and scanned the surrounding area. He had fallen back as we approached the castle and watched from afar as we explored it. I continued to look for him along the coast, knowing he was giving us our space.

Gentle motion by a large, flat boulder caught my eye. I focused on it and in an instant, I knew it wasn't Ryan.

Tears sprung to my eyes and my voice caught in my tightening throat.

"Oh my god," I whispered.

Paul and Rory followed my gaze off to the side and looked toward the boulder.

"My god!" Paul gasped and stumbled forward.

I hurried toward the figure at the rock, scrambling over wet stones and sliding over slippery sea grass as my heart pounded out of my chest. Rory and Paul raced after me with equal panic and determination.

The figure slumped across the surface of the boulder, and struggled to sit upright. Seaweed hung from the thin arms and dripped from the long brown hair.

My legs moved faster as I started to believe what my heart was telling me.

"Maeve!" I cried out.

She lifted her head in slow motion and blinked at us, supporting her weight on her shaking arms.

We ran to her, closing the distance between us as fast as possible. Terrified that she could disappear again at any moment.

"Oh my god, Maeve. Is it you?" I begged.

We slowed and moved closer to her with gentle caution. She squinted her eyes as if to see us better and studied each of our faces, pulling in every detail.

Slimy seaweed fell from her shoulder and she watched it splat on the rocks. Her exhausted gaze moved in and out of focus and she swayed and bobbed like she was about to pass out.

Paul moved up closer beside me and placed his hand on my shoulder for support. He leaned in and gazed into her face. A sound of overwhelmed anguish escaped his lips as he gasped and dropped to his knees, staring at her.

Rory remained riveted a step behind us, speechless and frozen as if he were seeing a ghost.

I looked over my shoulder and found Ryan far behind us. He stood at the edge of the castle, watching.

I nodded to him.

He was the witness.

Turning back to Maeve, I reached into my pocket and pulled out the pouch. I shook the ring into my palm and squeezed it with a silent prayer that it would work its miracles.

Without any sign of resistance, she let me take her hand and I pushed the ring onto her finger.

Her head reeled back and her mouth opened as if she were going to scream but instead a huge gasp escaped from her as she filled her lungs with life giving oxygen. She panted and pulled in another enormous breath that resonated across the rocky beach.

Her eyes brightened then and color returned to her face. She panted and propped herself to a stronger upright position. Swiping at the wet strands of hair that clung to her face, she pushed them aside and rubbed her eyes.

She looked at each of us and her lips quivered, preparing to speak.

"You two look like hell," she said to the guys with a raspy voice and a wicked smirk.

Their heads perked up in unison.

Then she gazed at me.

Her eyes lingered on me for a long while and then she finally spoke.

"Isobel," she said. "You've grown." She paused. "Grown into a warrior. I always knew you would."

EPILOGUE

Cups of tea ranneth over at Maureen's cottage as we gathered around her small table nibbling on scones, badgering Paul for more information about Maeve's condition and the security of the tomb at the clearing.

Maeve had been sheltered away by Rory and Paul and we didn't have immediate access to her which left us chomping for details. She initially needed immediate medical attention for malnutrition and dehydration, but their subtle hints about her need for time and space made it clear she struggled emotionally with the transition into her new world as well.

"The site is restricted now as a sacred burial ground. It will be protected by the government and left undisturbed," he told us.

"Thank Christ," Maureen blurted out.

"What about an investigation into Murt's disappearance? Is there any word on that?" I asked.

It had been a couple weeks now since the solstice and still there was no trace of him. Paul had tried to reach out to any friends or family but couldn't find anyone connected to him.

He was a traveler, biding his time, so it made sense he was a loner.

Colm was the only lead we had and he continued to seek forgiveness from Rory, writing Murt off completely. It was too late for him though; he'd already been blackballed by the clan.

"No. The police have nothing to go on. No body, no case." Paul placed his hands on the table. "But mind you, you don't think I'd just walk away from such a curiosity do you?"

I leaned in closer.

He continued. "I went down the hole on my own. Had to see for myself." He turned his mug in his hand. "I brought all my gear, you know, the excavation tools, and I discovered something very interesting."

Ryan shifted behind me, pressing into my chair. "What, man? You're killing us," he pleaded.

"The door that Murt saw lit up with dawn's light," he started.

"Yeah, that's the one he got sucked into," I said. "The one he thought was Maeve's. But it was the wrong one."

"Right," Paul agreed. "I inspected that door with all of my tools and electronic instruments and it was very clear to me. Clear that it hadn't been tampered with or opened in upward of five hundred years."

"What?" I spat some tea.

"I'm certain of it. The seal was intact. Undisturbed," Paul stated.

"That's not possible. I saw him jimmy it open. I watched him get sucked into it." My head shook in disbelief.

It was the mystical ways of the Druids. I'd witnessed their power at suppressing their enemy.

Unless...I tried to stifle my thoughts. *Unless his rogue order of Druids claimed him back through that portal.* My stomach dropped at the thought.

"Well," Maureen sighed. "Unfortunately, the Secret Society that Murt was a part of, they follow their own rules. Somethin' tells me we haven't seen the last of that bastard. And he'll be returning with a vengeance, no doubt."

Everyone fell silent at her words.

I prayed she was wrong, but as always, my gut knew she was right. Her sight and her intuition rang true every time. And now, it lined up with my premonition perfectly, assuring me that my truth sight was clear.

Paul stood and passed Maureen the folder of documents he brought for her regarding the ongoing excavation site on her property. He'd had the restrictions to the land legalized for her.

"Thank you, Paul." Maureen reached for the official papers. "For everything."

He looked into his empty mug and drew a shallow breath. "There's another reason I came to see ye."

I fixed my eyes on him without blinking.

"Patricia," he stated. "She knows Maeve is back now and she's out of her mind. It's as if she's been waiting for this day as long as we have." He coughed on his words. "Isobel, it's not safe for you now."

I stood from my seat in an uncontrollable flight response. "What do you mean?"

"Patricia figured out your escape from the institution." His eyes fell in defeat. "She came to my office again and explained her theory to me, step by step, and she wasn't far off the mark. She's the one obsessed now, you see." He lifted his eyes and looked straight into mine. "She plans to alert the authorities. It's only a matter of time before they catch up to you and they won't hesitate to throw you back in that prison."

My stomach dropped.

There was no way I could go back there. The thought of that hell hole haunted me to my core.

I closed my eyes and took a long inhale, reconnecting with my true inner self. My warrior self.

My eyes shot open then with a revelation that pounded my heart out of my chest.

"Let them," I stated.

"What?" Ryan blasted.

"Let them take me. I'll be ready." I drank the last of my tea.

"Ready for what?" Ryan snapped at me.

It was my next step. It was what I needed to do. And how else would I get back to that island? I might as well take a free ferry ride with Sister Goddamn Francis.

An inner grin lit me up from the inside. She had no idea what she would be getting herself into.

"Ready to rescue Jayne!" I blasted back with a huge smile that crossed my face.

Paul's jaw dropped and Ryan's brow pinched together.

Maureen stood and cleared the plates. "That's me girl." She slapped me on the back.

Her confidence in me set me standing taller.

"I'll just need a quick chat with Maeve first," I added. "Is she able to see me yet?"

Maeve had the ring.

She would have to be my accomplice in freeing Jayne. And something told me she'd be happy to do it. I just hoped she'd be ready.

Maybe this would be exactly what she needed to help with her adjustment to her new life. Keeping her gift alive would ensure her strength and purpose. And together, we could be a force.

The thought of working with Maeve awakened every nerve and charged every synapse in my body and I was certain others would see me glowing from my epiphany.

Paul put a hand up, ready to speak, but then hesitated as if reconsidering. After a moment, he looked at Ryan and me.

"I'm heading into town later to see her. And the Red King." He huffed. "He's with Maeve now, working through some clan history and chieftain details." He moved to the door. "Stop by if you like. I'd say she'd be ready for some new company outside of our two faces."

My heart rate accelerated. Seeing Maeve was now my immediate priority.

"Where?" I asked.

"The usual spot." He grinned. "Lynch's."

I looked over at Ryan for his reaction and watched intrigue brighten his eyes.

"We'll be there." I smiled.

~

After kissing Gram on the cheek, I raced toward the door. "I'll be back later. Declan and Michelle are joining us in town," I called to her.

"That's grand. Have fun, you two." Gram waved to Ryan and me as we pulled away in his truck.

We flew along the coast road into the city center and I bounced in my seat with excitement the entire way.

"Michelle's gonna crap herself," I said.

Ryan smiled and nodded as he pulled into a spot by the Spanish Arch. We walked along the bridge toward Quay Street and found Michelle and Declan at the river's edge by the swans.

We chattered our way up toward Shop Street and a twinge of guilt poked at my ribs for keeping Declan and Michelle in the dark about Maeve's return.

I had to protect them though. The less they knew, the better. In case there was an inquiry of any kind.

But now, it was time to pull them back into the loop. Michelle's close friendship to Maeve could be therapeutic for Maeve's transition. It would help her to feel more herself again.

We approached Lynch's Pub and Michelle grabbed onto my arm.

"I love this place! I used to come here all the time. We'd come to see Rory's band way back when," she reminisced.

And I knew she used to come here with Maeve.

I pushed the door open and led her in. A few patrons gathered at the bar, but the tables were empty, except for the one nestled under the ancient stone arch at the back.

Declan and Ryan followed us as we made our way deeper into the quiet pub.

Paul's head lifted first and his bright smile greeted us. Rory's eyes widened when he saw us approaching and he stood in surprise at seeing Michelle. Without hesitation, he stepped away from the table a bit, exposing the girl who sheltered behind him.

Maeve sat in the shadows of the great stone arch, still adjusting to her new existence—a second chance at life, basically—and she slowly lifted her head.

She smiled at me and then looked to Michelle.

Their eyes met at exactly the same moment and they froze in each other's wide-eyed gazes.

"Maeve?" Michelle's voice shook out of her in disbelief as her hand flew to her mouth.

And she collapsed into my arms.

I fanned Michelle's face as she slept, propped on our jackets against the wall in the pub. I couldn't blame her for shutting down completely from the shock. But how else do you tell someone their best friend has returned from the dead?

"I've missed her." Maeve smirked. Color filled her cheeks as she gazed at Michelle's slumped form.

Then her face grew serious and she sat up taller.

"I need to warn you, Isobel." She turned to me with a somber expression that chilled my blood. "It's not over."

Rory and Paul shot stares at her that screamed of feeling left out of the loop. She'd clearly been withholding information from them.

Everyone leaned in closer to hear her muffled words.

She continued, "They won't accept defeat. It's not in their nature."

I leaned in closer to hear every syllable of what she was saying as my heart rate plummeted to my feet.

"What the hell does that mean?" Ryan barked.

I reached my hand toward him, to quiet his outburst.

"In the Druid's cavern, the altar…" she started.

I interrupted her. "Yes. It's a time portal. I know. I was able to decode its hidden instructions, Maeve. The equations are embedded within the carvings. I know how to use it!"

Paul pulled back in surprise.

"Excellent." She lowered her eyes in relief. "That's exactly what we'll need."

"Need for what?" Paul blurted in frustration. "We're sealing off the tomb. No more entry." His hands spread out in front of him like he was creating a barrier.

Maeve's eyes moved to Paul briefly but then focused back on me.

"There are other travelers," she stated. "You weren't the first to decipher the code of the time portal, Isobel."

Everyone's breathing stopped, anticipating Maeve's next words.

"Its creators. They are the ones who'll stop at nothing. They won't end their quest. Ever." Her voice grew louder with each passing word. "It is their one true purpose, to stop the progress of time. And they won't allow anyone to stop them."

But then, she gazed off and stared into space as if watching a movie. Her breathing became short and shallow.

Her hands trembled as she pushed herself back from the table, staring at us as if we were in danger.

Then she spoke with a low, shaky tone.

"Isobel. They are coming for us."

The end.

AFTERWORD

I hope you enjoyed book two of the Irish Mystic Legends series, Curse Raider. For a sneak peek at a teaser from book three, Truth Seer, click a few pages and you will find it. Be sure to visit my website for more information and buy links.

Thank you!

www.jenniferrosemcmahon.com

To sign up for my newsletter:
https://www.subscribepage.com/f1p9w6

ACKNOWLEDGMENTS

Thank you to Naomi Hughes for her amazing editing super powers and for supporting my growth as an author through seven books, so far!

Thank you to my family for all the love and support around what it takes to write books. Love to the McMahon Clan and the O'Malley Clan. :)

TRUTH SEER TEASER

We promised we wouldn't come back here.

They said it was too dangerous and best to leave the mystical burial chamber undisturbed.

And we had agreed, whole-heartedly. At first.

But then, our true natures took over--jinxed with curiosity and conjuring, gifted with extrasensory experiences that went beyond what some would call witchcraft or black magic. We were more in the realm of full-blown ancient Druid curse.

So we couldn't be blamed for our defiance. We couldn't help ourselves.

I squeezed Maeve's hand as we moved through the darkness of the subterranean catacombs. My racing heart led the way while the beams of light from our phones illuminated ancient artifacts intended to be left unseen for all of time.

We'd come to explore the secret burial chamber further. Just the two of us this time, to search for clues of the coming of the assassin Druids which Maeve had seen in a recent, disturbing vision. And to explore the ancient carvings on the elusive altar, a portal of some form, with its hidden secrets.

But we also came to visit Maeve's final resting place, nestled within the numerous alcoves of peace. She had to see it for herself to truly believe that her legendary journey to the past had come full circle.

The massive stone statues of the guardians, the Keepers of the Ovates, didn't flinch when we crept out of the narrow passageway leading down into the sacred tomb. Their job was to guard the catacombs, but also to protect the seers—the honorable, gifted Druids. And I was one of them—newly initiated, with the nervous-twitch-PTSD to prove it.

It was as if the guardians expected us, with their wide eyes and haunting expressions, showing off their adept skill at scaring off unwanted intruders. But for us, they granted safe passage.

Did they expect our murderous trackers as well, though? Did they know we were being followed?

At the solstice, ending the ancient curse on the progression of time, set by the deviant Druid clan, hadn't been enough to stop their aggressive pursuit of us. Maeve had seen it in her shocking vision that turned everything we believed on its head. We thought the curse had ended. But she saw different. The rogue Druids had a back-up plan to reinstate a stronger plague, one that couldn't be easily broken. It involved unyielding victory. Damnation.

And that absolute victory was attainable in only one way.

Stopping us.

Dead in our tracks.

We moved through the dank, echoing tunnel into the silent sanctuary of the burial chamber. My mind awakened with the ancient knowledge of millennia that filled the sacred space. The information that had been revealed to me during the ritual of the solstice had tapped into parts of my brain I hadn't known existed and complex images of time overlapping on itself whirled in my head without rest. The source of that infinite knowledge of the time continuum, the stone altar, stood solid in the center of the chamber, surrounded by alcoves filled with skulls, long bones, and small doors concealing the stillness of final rest.

Celtic carvings along the sides of the mystical altar danced in our light beams, drawing us closer. My hand moved along the symbols and intricacies of the ancient dead language, but then I lifted my fingers from the grooves. Following the etchings of their elusive code could activate the power of the portal, or worse, conjure a jarring vision that might launch us back into the abyss.

The altar was a vulnerability and a danger. What if the enemy Druids knew its power too? What if they understood its ability to facilitate time travel? The tiny hairs on the back of my neck stood up. Of course they understood it. It was created in their time. The time of divine mysticism and supernatural magic.

"Isobel. Which one is mine?" Maeve turned to the catacomb vaults, moving her eyes along the numerous burial chamber doors and crevices.

My thoughts jolted back to our mission and my throat constricted from the thought of what Maeve must be feeling. Her two worlds colliding, past and present.

I stepped to the small door that had been revealed weeks earlier by dawn's light on the day of the solstice. The ray of golden light had lit up the secret location, hidden among numerous similar chambers, showing me where Maeve's final resting place lay.

But, when it had popped open in the mystifying dawn light, her chamber was devoid of any evidence of a body. The only item within her crypt was a small box that held the ring.

The ring of the pirate queen.

And that relic was exactly what had been needed to bring Maeve back through the portal of time.

Back home to us.

It had been placed there five hundred years earlier with the hope, or plan, that it would be found at just the right time. And that time was the solstice. It had been predicted in the Book of Druids as the most sacred time of year.

And it proved to be true.

I'd come of age, finally, and found myself in the tomb that day straining to make contact with her. To pull her out of the abyss. Delivering her back to her original life here.

But I knew she still struggled with the complexities of her leap through the dimensions of the time continuum, not knowing which realm was truly hers. She had lived her life hundreds of years earlier, by choice, but had now returned, six years later from the date she disappeared from our sight.

That day, six years ago, was the day I grew up. Or more specifically, woke up.

I watched her wandering through the catacombs as I remembered that moment six years earlier when she disappeared into the mist. The time when I realized my own curse couldn't be ignored any more. The moment I knew it was real and I, too, could become lost in the abyss. Maybe forever.

Maeve reached for the aged limestone door of her burial chamber and ran her hand over it. Her eyes closed as she made contact with her own death.

Then her eyes widened in surprise.

"There's a carving here," she said as she rubbed the small door. "Too dull to see." She closed her eyes again and traced the carving with her finger. "I recognize it," she gasped. "It's a symbol I created when I was in the deep past at Rockfleet. Two hearts intertwined as Celtic knots."

I nodded my head in understanding. I'd seen that carving before too. Maeve revealed it to me in an earlier vision--like an attempt to help me find her hidden resting place. And ultimately, to find the ring that had the power to bring her back.

When the light of dawn on the solstice had illuminated her chamber door, I felt the subtle carvings on its surface too and knew it to be the right one. I'd never forget the relief that poured through me when there was no evidence of a body within; no bones, nothing. It confirmed to me that she was still out there. Trapped in the void. Alive.

"The only thing inside your chamber was a small box," I mumbled. "It held the ring." My voice stuck then and struggled to leave my mouth. "When you...back at Rockfleet...at the end. They said you just faded away. That there was nothing to bury. You were just...gone."

She paused with her hand on the stone hatch of her grave, remembering.

"How do you know that?" she muttered.

I thought back to the words of the Immortal Druid. "A messenger had been waiting here for me. He called me the truth seer."

Her hand fell from her burial chamber door.

"Truth seer?" She paused and then exhaled. "Yes. I suppose I knew that about you." She nodded in understanding.

"Well, I sure didn't. Kinda took me by surprise." I thought about it for a second. "Or not."

She then shifted back to the topic of her 'death'. "Faded?" she repeated. "Like, no body?" She looked back at the burial door. "It must have been a part of my crossing over, Isobel. I moved into the abyss of our visions. The void of time." Her face fell. "It was as if I was trapped. For what could have become eternity."

Shades of sorrow darkened her eyes as if proving how much she grieved for her life at Rockfleet. For her true love, Rí.

I had no idea how she would accomplish her transition back to the present--to her original life, after everything she had experienced in the deep past, five hundred years earlier; real happiness and belonging.

And it scared me.

I was afraid she would never transition back. Never find true happiness again.

But more so, I feared for my own life too.

The Druids were coming for us with a vengeance that burned in their souls. They were coming to take the only life I knew and now, finally, loved. The thought of it being taken from me, through the misguided action and greed of others, terrified me deep in my bones.

But for Maeve, it was a second chance at life now. Could she embrace it and make it work? Or would she be forever trapped in grief and longing for what she once knew and loved?

I moved back to the altar, refocusing on searching for clues. Anything to give us information on how or when the ancient Druids would be coming for us.

Tracking us through time, their evil intent was clear from Maeve's vision.

To end us.

Stopping them, and the deep-routed curse, was critical if I wanted to continue to live my life the way it was. The way it was meant to be.

And I did.

I loved the people around me. I wanted to be with Ryan, completely. I wanted to share time with everyone I cared about—Declan and Michelle. Gram. Mother Maureen. And my true friends. The ones who all put themselves on the line to help me. Every time.

Of all the people we'd left uniformed, if my brother Declan found out I'd come here again, he'd freakin' kill me. His protective nature was like Fort Knox and he couldn't handle it for even a second when I tampered with my second sight.

Maeve stepped back from her burial chamber with a stumble, as the shade of emotional green moved over her face. Within two seconds, she was hunched over, dry-heaving at the stone floor.

I jumped to her and rubbed her trembling back as she wretched with convulsing shakes. I pulled her hair back away from her face as she spat out her emotional overload.

Crumbling to the floor, she shuddered from the violent, empty wretches. Then dropped her head into her knees and she rocked in self-soothing rhythm.

I reached around her shoulders and held tight in an attempt to hold her together.

"It's a lot, Maeve," I whispered. "You have to give yourself time to adjust back."

She lifted her head slightly and the glow of my phone illuminated the side of her face.

"I don't know, Izzy." She gazed at the door of her resting place. "I was happy there. It was…different. Everything mattered. And everyone. They mattered." She flipped her phone around in her hand. "The clan. It was like a tight-knit family and we all relied on each other. We needed each other." She hesitated. "There's a loneliness in our existence now. Here. And I can't help but think these psycho Druids have a point."

I turned my light beam directly on her. "What are you talking about?"

"They predicted the future would be like this," she said. "Cold. Detached. Broken." She squinted into my light. "They want to keep the magic and the mysticism of the past alive."

"But, Maeve, what they are planning is murder." My voice cracked with tension. "And it's more than just preserving the beauty of the past. They want power. It's no different from the dictators of the modern world. Power hungry to control the world around them. But instead of man-made nuclear weapons and modern terrorism, they are tapping into the natural sources of the infinite universe—time itself."

"I know. You're right." Her head dropped again. "The times are just so vastly different, between Rockfleet and now. I can't help but ache for that feeling again. Of love. And camaraderie."

Her voice caught in her throat as it tightened and I knew she fought tears. Her love for Rí was deep in her soul and her experience at Rockfleet was full and profound. But she was here now. And we had to fight for what we had, what was possible, and for our futures.

I felt the camaraderie and support she was speaking of in my own life. I felt it in the people I surrounded myself with and I had to help her feel it again too. It could sometimes get lost in the static and chaos of modern life, but it still existed.

Searching all around me, not knowing what else to say or do, I stared into the darkness of the catacomb. Moving my hands along the dusty floor in nervous motion, my fingers trailed through indentations and imperfections in the stone slab beneath us.

I traced the curves and swirls over and over and then gasped.

There was a repeating pattern.

Hopping up to my feet, I stepped back and shone my light on the floor around Maeve. She looked up at me through heavy eyes that brightened with curiosity. Moving further back, my eyes widened as an entire slab of ancient carvings presented itself beneath us.

"Look!" I blurted. "All around you. It's a language of some kind. Sentences. Like a list." My eyes darted along the systematic structure of the ancient etchings.

Maeve jumped to her feet with renewed vigor and stepped off the carvings on the slab. Then she bent down, squinting her eyes for a better look and pressed her finger along some of the grooves.

She shot up to her full height then and stared at me. As if being choked by her words, she fought to spit them out, one by one, in sounds that brittled my bones.

With terror in her gaze, she whispered, "The prophecies."

#

Her harrowing words set my spine rigid. They carried warning and ancient mystery that generated the unnerving feel of judgment day all around me.

"Prophecies?" I stepped further away from the carved slab for fear of conjuring something. "What the hell does that mean?"

Maeve knelt for a better look and traced some more of the indentations as if reading Braille.

"The prophecies of the ancient, honorable Druids," she mumbled while attempting to read them more thoroughly. "Predicting the coming of the rogue clan of the Secret Order."

"The bad guys coming?" I stepped further away from the carvings, knowing the evil intent of the Secret Order. They were the ones coming for us. Terrorists from the deep past.

She nodded, moving her fingers toward the beginning of the carvings.

"They're a warning," she murmured. "A list of signs, basically, predicting the coming of the deviant clan. The Soldiers of Death, they're called here." She tapped on a line of mystical carvings.

"So, these were written by the good guys?" I bent my head for a better look.

"Yes," Maeve replied. "They're basically warning us. Foretelling..." She paused.

"Foretelling what?" I begged.

She examined the carvings further and then pulled back in fear. "The coming of dooms day."

I stepped back again until I pressed against the far wall of the catacombs. My heart pounded in my chest as I tried to steady my erratic breathing.

It was really happening.

Maeve saw them coming in her vision, but here it was right in front of us. Etched in stone from thousands of years ago. Ancient prophecies predicting the arrival of our hunters. Forecasting the end of the world.

"How could this still be happening?" I kicked my foot at the carvings on the floor. "How could they have known that we stopped their original attempt? We ended their curse at the solstice. But somehow they knew it would fail and so they were prepared to try again. How could that be?" I pleaded.

It was true. The ancient Druids held the knowledge that we stopped their original curse. As if someone had alerted them to the events that unfolded at the solstice a few weeks ago. They knew their curse failed and so they put a second plan into motion, thousands of years ago. But how could they have known?

Now, with that leaked knowledge, they had planned their final attack.

A full-scale, deliberate assault on the modern world. Mass annihilation.

Dooms day.

But also a brutal, direct attack on us, their enemy. We were the target that had the power to stop them. And they knew it. We'd done it once already.

So now, they were coming for us.

Tracking us through the wormholes of time in a final attempt to protect their insidious curse and allow it to come to fruition.

"Their power runs deep through the rhythms of the earth," Maeve said through clenched teeth. "And they aim to take control of the ultimate force; the power of time itself. Nothing can stop them."

I stared at the intricate designs on the altar, the ones that had revealed to me the secrets of controlled time travel. I had been foolish to think I was the only one who had decoded and understood their mystery.

"So, if we don't exist, they would have sole authority on the progression of time?" I asked.

Maeve nodded.

It made sense.

If they killed Maeve and me, they would stop our ability to move through time with our visions and eradicate their wrongful abuse of the portal. They wanted absolute control over it, to twist time to their preferred goal; preserving Gaelic Ireland and stopping modernization.

My knees buckled beneath me at the thought of my unseen stalkers--cloaked misanthropes from another time with a vengeance to kill for what they believed in.

But I was the truth seer.

A modern, honorable Druid.

My initiation into Druidry and my enlightenment from the ritual of the solstice had to mean more. It could guide me through this. It had to.

But how?

We needed to survive their attack before they could gain the opportunity at reinstating their curse. That was the priority at the moment.

My hands ran through my hair, squeezing my skull to keep it from exploding. I felt like a sitting duck, exposed and waiting for my killer to appear at any time.

Maeve turned her phone and took pictures of the floor from a variety of angles, brushing dust and sand off specific areas to expose more writing.

Satisfied she'd captured enough for us to interpret later, she leaned back with me against the wall and we stared at the designs on the floor as if they might begin speaking to us.

"As the prophecies occur, one by one, they'll warn us of the coming of the Druids as they get closer." She scrolled through her photos of the carvings, then zoomed in on the last shot. "This one, it looks like the final sign."

She tapped on her screen as I gazed into the light of her phone, focusing on what looked like a depiction of the sun and the moon, then a blending of the two.

"An eclipse," I stated.

"Yes. A unique eclipse," she replied, zooming in on more markings. "These are numbers. Dates, maybe. In the thousands." She looked back to the floor to compare accuracy. "I think they mean that this type of eclipse only occurs every couple thousand years." She paused. "Basically, it's our deadline."

I grimaced at her poor word choice and a squeak escaped my throat as I swallowed. I hadn't heard news of an impending eclipse, but I rarely paid attention to astrological events, aside from the recent solstice, anyway.

Just as I found my voice, a strange vibration ran through my back, causing me to flinch. Maeve jolted too. Then an unnerving crunching sound of stone rubbing on stone rumbled at our feet.

And then it moved.

The wall behind us sank in a few inches exposing a massive panel in the wall that shifted, opening a hidden space behind it with a deep groan. The eerie sound turned to guttural moans that wafted up to us from the depths of hell.

Jumping back, we fumbling with the flashlights on our phones and aimed our beams into the dark passage within the wall. My heart beat pounded in my ears but not loud enough to block the terrifying sound of Maeve's hyperventilating breaths.

"Shit. What is that?" I choked on my words. "A secret passage?"

The light from my phone shook from the trembling of my hand.

We inched closer, pressing our shoulders together, and peered into the dark crevice.

"A hidden chamber?" Maeve whispered.

The light from our phones was too weak to illuminate the vast darkness of the space behind the wall and we strained see further in.

I pressed my hand against the solid stone panel and with the slightest pressure, it moved further open without a sound.

"Oh my god. We can fit through," I gasped.

But then my hand flew to my face as a waft of ancient stench hit me between the eyes, turning my stomach.

Maeve choked. "Jesus." And she wretched. "It's like the air of a thousand-year-old grave."

And just in that instant, our phones went dead, leaving us in pitch darkness.

The moaning from within the secret chamber grew louder and the rancid stench overwhelmed us, sending us stumbling back. Just as we steadied ourselves, a fluttering sound escaped the secret passage. The fluttering grew in intensity to a level of thunderous vibration and pounding that sent immediate panic through me.

Something was coming. Something big.

And in that instant, pure terror took over.

I grabbed for Maeve's arm through the darkness.

"Run!"

ABOUT THE AUTHOR

Jennifer Rose McMahon is a USA Today Bestselling Author who has been creating her Pirate Queen series and Irish Mystic Legends series since her college days abroad in Ireland. Her passion for Irish legends, ancient cemeteries, and medieval ghost stories has fueled her adventurous story telling, while her husband's decadent brogue carries her imagination through the centuries. When she's not in her own world writing about castles and curses, she can be found near Boston in the local coffee shop, yoga studio, or at the beach...most often answering to the name 'Mom' by her fab children four.

www.jenniferrosemcmahon.com
info@jenniferrosemcmahon.com

ALSO BY JENNIFER ROSE MCMAHON

Pirate Queen Series

Bohermore

Inish Clare

Ballycroy

Rockfleet, Prequel

Irish Mystic Legends Series

Legend Hunter

Curse Raider

Truth Seer

www.ingramcontent.com/pod-product-compliance
Lightning Source LLC
Chambersburg PA
CBHW030309200626
46816CB00002BA/828

9780997077926